G R JORDAN

The Guilty Parties

A Highlands and Islands Detective Thriller

First edition

ISBN: 978-1-915562-42-5

This book was professionally typeset on Reedsy.
Find out more at reedsy.com

The worst guilt is to accept an un-earned guilt.

AYN RAND

Contents

Foreword

The events of this book, while based around real locations in the north of Scotland, are entirely fictional and all characters do not represent any living or deceased person. All companies are fictitious representations.

Acknowledgement

To Ken, Jean, Colin, Evelyn, John and Rosemary for your work in bringing this novel to completion, your time and effort is deeply appreciated.

Novels by G R Jordan

The Highlands and Islands Detective series (Crime)

1. Water's Edge
2. The Bothy
3. The Horror Weekend
4. The Small Ferry
5. Dead at Third Man
6. The Pirate Club
7. A Personal Agenda
8. A Just Punishment
9. The Numerous Deaths of Santa Claus
10. Our Gated Community
11. The Satchel
12. Culhwch Alpha
13. Fair Market Value
14. The Coach Bomber
15. The Culling at Singing Sands
16. Where Justice Fails
17. The Cortado Club
18. Cleared to Die
19. Man Overboard!
20. Antisocial Behaviour
21. Rogues' Gallery
22. The Death of Macleod - Inferno Book 1

Kirsten Stewart Thrillers (Thriller)

Jac Moonshine Thrillers

The Contessa Munroe Mysteries (Cozy Mystery)

1. Corpse Reviver
2. Frostbite
3. Cobra's Fang

The Patrick Smythe Series (Crime)

1. The Disappearance of Russell Hadleigh
2. The Graves of Calgary Bay
3. The Fairy Pools Gathering

Austerley & Kirkgordon Series (Fantasy)

1. Crescendo!
2. The Darkness at Dillingham
3. Dagon's Revenge
4. Ship of Doom

Supernatural and Elder Threat Assessment Agency (SETAA) Series (Fantasy)

1. Scarlett O'Meara: Beastmaster

Island Adventures Series (Cosy Fantasy Adventure)

1. Surface Tensions

Dark Wen Series (Horror Fantasy)

1. The Blasphemous Welcome
2. The Demon's Chalice

Chapter 01

Tom Balshaw sat over his glass of red wine, staring at the gathered multitude in front of him. If he counted, there would be twelve tables, all with at least eight people sat around them. Lunch had been impressive, for it was quite something to have lobster served on an occasion such as this. Then again, this was the big leagues.

Tom was there representing one small branch of the overall corporation. Allen Brothers, that was the umbrella, and the Allens were there. Tom's own operation, Y-Cliffe Wonders, was one of the smaller parts, but his numbers had been good, and he'd been invited along.

The Allens had been presenting some awards for those who had done particularly well. While the Allens never gave out notice of who was receiving what, to have simply been invited meant Tom must be in with a good chance. He was also away from the family for at least a few days, and he was tired. The last couple of years had been tough. He'd driven the business, spending many hours out of the house, and then when he came back, it was constant. The kids needed this; the baby needed that. *She was tired.* He was tired, too. He was running a business; didn't she understand that?

That was the whole point of her being there—to run the house. I mean, he hadn't married her for her brain, after all. No, she was good on his arm, and now she'd have to get good at running a household. That was her job. There was no doubt he was the flash one in this partnership. That was Tom.

The downside of having the kids was Laura had gone off the boil. When they initially married, she had been attentive to his needs but not anymore. Now she wasn't in the mood. Now she wasn't this; she wasn't that. Just because she had kids didn't mean her duties towards him had ceased.

He'd even got her help. That little Portuguese woman came in twice a week. He remembered when they'd sat down, tried to figure out some assistance. The Portuguese woman had been more expensive. She was also older, but, in truth, she was good at what she did. She seemed to have a way with the kids.

But there had been that younger one. Sarah, just out of college, a swimmer, and her toned body told all that. Tom reckoned she'd smiled too much, flashed her eyes towards him. His wife, Anna, wouldn't have it. Pity, as he would have had Sarah.

'You're not bringing a hussy in here. She was practically wanting to take you to bed with those eyes.'

Well, that was true. Sarah was clearly up for it. The Portuguese woman was different. Tom couldn't even say her name, but one thing about her was she wasn't going to bed with Tom, not at her age. He had standards, after all.

The downside of this conference was he'd had to bring his sister with him, mainly because she worked hard within the business and was a co-director. She was constantly telling Tom that he was lucky to have found Anna, but what did she know? Trust her to take the woman's side. Anyway, one day Anna would get fed up and leave. That's what will happen.

He looked at Peter from the bathroom furnishings company. His wife had left him, but only when he made all that money, only when she could rob him of half of it. That's the trouble with the courts. They don't understand who really built up businesses, and that was why Tom decided it would be okay if he played around a bit.

He wasn't one of those people who believed in true love, not one of those people who believed in a lifetime of commitment. Anna would leave him one day. She'd take him for all he had, so on the way, he'd have some fun. He gazed around and caught the eye of that rather attractive brunette from the spirit's division of Allen's drinks concern.

Allison Burnage. She may have been forty, but she was a forty-year-old with a bit of sass, and a lot of it had been pointed towards Tom the previous evening. She'd left just a little too early, but today would be different. He watched as her red lips smiled at him, and she wandered over with a glass of wine casually swinging in her hand.

The dress she wore was elegant, but it was cut specifically, showing just enough to keep a man like Tom hanging, the leg coming out the side. She was also in fine fettle, clearly a woman who worked hard to keep her figure.

That was another thing about Anna. *Too much time with the kids. I don't have time for working out. I don't have time to keep in shape. My food's my own to choose.* Sounded more like a lack of commitment to Tom. What the hell; if she would not make the effort, he'd find someone else, and Allison looked like the right person.

She plonked herself in the seat beside Tom, placing the glass

3

of wine on the white sheet that covered the table, but the glass tipped slightly. A drop of wine flew out from the top and Tom watched it spatter, seeping into the perfect tablecloth.

'Whoops,' said Allison. 'Had a few too many of those.'

'I don't think you've had enough,' said Tom. He watched as she laughed. She clearly had drunk a few because the laugh was over the top, but she leaned forward and whispered in his ear.

'I could share a bottle with you, but somewhere warm and comfortable.'

'All right,' said Tom. It looked like tonight was on. He sat back in his seat, an enormous smile across his face, and reached up and undid his shirt, allowing his tie to hang loose. He felt himself getting a little warm and more than a little turned on by this turn of events. Her smile, with hair flowing down either side of her face, promised much, but something behind her caught Tom's eye.

The conference meal was taking place in a large hall on an estate in the Cairngorms. It was a very private function, and the company liked it that way because at night, it meant none of their people embarrassed themselves in the towns or cities. What went on at these conferences stayed at these conferences. Those who ran these things understood they were far away from everyone, but with a level of luxury not found elsewhere.

There was a buzz in the hall, for after the meal, Mr Allen would speak, and he'd dish out the awards. Nobody knew who would win, so everyone was excited. If you were here, you had a chance, and if you won, who knew what business you could take over or how far up the ranks you could get. The Allens were tough people, but they rewarded success.

The air was changing now, and Tom saw a group of people

4

walk in with several large plastic-looking suitcases. Maybe they were musicians' crates. Whatever they were, they were mainly plastic in design. Stout, though, and a group of about ten men, at least Tom assumed they were men, were setting them down. What bothered Tom was that their faces seemed to be covered. They wore large hoods under black jackets. All wore black Janes as well.

Tom watched as the group moved in and started taking the boxes around the different parts of the room. Something was bothering him, and as they walked, they all seemed to stop at the exits. There were four out of this hall. One where the men had come in. There were large double doors that led out to the reception area. A small door led out to the side, more of a fire door than anything else. Finally, another one that led up to rooms within the hotel.

Tom wondered what the men were doing and watched as they opened the plastic cases. The large double doors that led out to reception were suddenly covered; a cloth draped across them. Drills were produced, attaching the cloth to a wooden plinth, and completely blocking any view to the outside. Doors seemed to be locked, and Tom could see that the rest of the crowd inside had got a bit suspicious of what was going on. Was this one of Alan's tricks? They were known for it, known to put their people through the grinder.

Tom took a drink of his wine and looked back at Allison before him. She must have been drunk, for she had noticed nothing going on. Instead, she just smiled at him, her hand reaching forward and running up the side of his thigh. Normally he would have engaged with her completely, even seen if he could take her up to the room early, or popped outside for a bit of exercise. However, with what was going

5

on, he was feeling a little worried.

Tom suddenly clocked one figure as it took off the jacket he was wearing. He threw it on the floor, and pulled up his grey top, yanking the bottom out of his trousers. This revealed a full monk's habit, and he allowed it to fall down to the ankles. The man looked across at him, and Tom saw the face was masked, almost grey and robotic, resembling a person, but not in the finer details. He had seen that before. They'd been on the television.

He stood up, trying to back away, and fell over the chair.

'Are you all right?' asked Allison. 'Let me help you.' She stumbled forward, fell over Tom, and landed on her back. Tom got to his feet, and his heart thudded as two shots were fired up into the ceiling. He saw two figures who had come in were now dressed in their monk's habits and had guns.

'Right, everyone down on your knees,' cried a voice. 'If you don't, you'll be dead. I'll count to three. One.'

Tom was on the ground, but rolled onto his knees, putting his hands behind his head. This seemed serious. He had seen that face before. It had been on the television, the news. It had been that time when they'd, dear God, when they'd killed that clergyman. He shook.

'Two.'

Allison was stumbling back up to her feet. She was walking this way and that, and Tom shouted at her to get down. Around him was chaos. People stumbling this way and that.

'Three.'

Tom went to reach for Allison to pull her down to her knees, but she spun, hitting the ground and not moving, blood pouring out of the side of her head. There were a couple more shots and people screamed.

'I said I would count to three, and then I would shoot. Well, some people don't count well. Right. Some of you will get out of here alive because you have done nothing wrong. Well, you work for this evil corporation, but maybe you don't know how bad they've been. Some of you do, and some of you are going to pay.'

Tom saw not all the figures were training guns on the people. Four of them were pulling stanchions out of boxes. They worked quickly, and soon several small portable gallows had been erected. Tom counted five.

'Some of you may wonder where the money from Allen Brothers came from. Mr Allen knows, and if he stands up now and lets us know, we might let him live. Of course, we're filming all of this, filming it so we can get through to the public. Corporations like Allen Brothers need to be taken out. They are leeches. It's not good business.

Tom watched as Mr Allen, resplendent in a white tuxedo, was hauled up to the gallows. A noose was put around his neck, and he was made to stand on a chair from the conference.

'Any words, Mr Allen?' Sweat poured off the man, but he remained silent.

'Oh, well,' said the man in the habit, 'I will enjoy this. Let's see. Yes, your brother, your nephew. Oh, your sister, of course. She's one of the worst . . . and oh, yes, your aunt.'

'Goodness' sake, man,' shouted Mr Allen suddenly. 'She's ninety-two.'

'And she's been at this longer than you have. That woman should have seen a jail cell three or four times over. Well, she'll meet God today. See what he thinks of her.'

Tom was motionless with fear as he watched figures bring each of the Allens up to their individual gallows and put nooses around their necks. The frames were cold, metallic-like scaffolding, and the ropes so simple, but the scene was horrific.

'Anything to say? Are you going to let the police work this one out?'

The grey figure in a monk's habit who was striding around running the commentary, turned for a moment and looked at Tom. He could barely see the eyes through the mask, but they were penetrating. The figure walked over to him, grabbed the hair behind his head, and pulled his neck back.

'You been involved with this lot long?' said the figure.

'No,' said Tom, lying through his teeth.

'Don't worry. I know all about you, Tom. You are qualified to watch this. You just haven't quite got it in you to be up amongst the gallows. Not far off though, Tom.'

The man smacked Tom with the back of his hand, then drove the butt of his gun into Tom's face, sending him to the floor. Tom covered his face, feeling the blood pouring out, but somebody grabbed him and hauled him back up to his knees.

'On your knees, please,' said the man. 'I want everybody to watch this. Well, I wanted everybody. Alas, a few of them seem to have left early,' said the man, motioning to Allison's body lying beside Tom.

'On behalf of all people who are decent, on behalf of everyone you guys have screwed over physically, morally, financially, I hereby sentence you all to death. Oh, and with extreme pain.'

The man walked up to Allen, took something out, and drove a knife up into the man's stomach. When he retracted it, the grey monk kicked the chair away, and Tom watched Allen's body fall, and his neck half snap. The man continued down

8

the line, doing exactly the same to each member of the family. The man in the grey monk's habit then walked over to the camera that was filming the entire event.

'Try to work it out,' he said. 'You boys in blue, try to work it out. They're deserving of it. I want you to find it out for yourselves. I want you to tell everyone because this won't be the last.'

Tom watched as guns were kept trained on the crowd. Both boxes were packed up, and as quickly as they'd come in, ten monks disappeared back out the side door. He looked across at the body of Allison and felt his own body shaking. The blood was still coming down from his face, and tears were involuntarily coming to him. He'd almost died. Almost died.

There was no screaming in the room. People were running over to those who had been on the gallows. Someone hauled down the curtains that obscured the lobby. People were reaching for phones to call the police.

Tom stood up, looked down at Allison with regret, and then glanced across at Allen swinging on his gallows. Well, that promotion was screwed, wasn't it? 'Bugger,' said Tom. He reached for a bottle of wine, poured himself another large glass, and turned to Allison.

'Would've been great, love.' He downed the liquid.

Chapter 02

Macleod sat down, sweat running off the back of his neck. He wasn't accustomed to this much dancing, but Jane deserved it. She'd put up with a lot of issues over the last while—his grumpiness, his anger at not having caught the killers that had dispatched three ministers and nearly got their hands on another two.

His mind had been caught up on them. He'd been elsewhere, not attentive to her. They'd gone on holiday, and he barely noticed where they'd been. The grey monks had been gnawing at him. A piece of unfinished business, a file that couldn't be closed, but here was a joyous occasion.

It had been four months since Clarissa had left the office at the police station, saying yes to a man from the golf club. Only four months to plan and execute a wedding, but then again, Macleod knew Clarissa. She could do anything she put her mind to, except perhaps come back to being a police officer. She'd walked that day, told them all that she couldn't take it, told them all that she was sick of it. He couldn't blame her.

She had seen Patterson go down. Clarissa had held his throat, praying to God for an ambulance, praying she could keep him alive. And she had. Patterson owed his life to her. Even if

10

the man wasn't back on the force yet, he was alive. He'd have trauma, serious mental trauma from the situation. So would Clarissa.

She'd refused help from the police force, from the counsellors that Macleod tried to line up for her. She wouldn't take any of it, desperate to be away from the place. He had pondered if he had been wise to bring her in. Was she the right option? She was an integral part of the team, though. Of that, Macleod was sure, but technically, it was now Hope's decision if they were going to replace Clarissa. Hope's decision, in conjunction with medical staff and HR, whether Clarissa would even be fit enough to come back.

A figure landed in the seat beside him. The long red hair swinging around in an unfamiliar fashion. Macleod had seen Hope so often with a ponytail that he swore that was the way her hair came. Tonight, she had let it out, and she was in excellent form. She needed this. They'd all needed this, something to celebrate. Clarissa's marriage had been one tangible moment of joy to get hold of.

The church service had been splendid. Flowers down the aisle, everything decorated, and one thrilled woman who, in fairness, still stomped up the aisle. She didn't walk that steadily, former injuries coming to the fore. She looked well considering her age. There was a fortunate man at the front of the aisle and Macleod thought he was well-suited to her. The groundsman from the golf club was quiet, thoughtful, and very patient.

Macleod had also managed to get Clarissa's green sports car restored. The insurance had been a pain but he'd made it a personal mission, an attempt to bring a little joy back to her from the situation. It had pleased her but she remained distant about work.

Macleod had got the feeling that Clarissa had been avoiding him today, though. She never gave him more than the briefest of smiles. When he went over to give his congratulations, she had turned away, not rudely but hurrying off to some other engagement. He was a police officer. He noticed these things, and she was definitely shunning him.

'Well, well, you certainly hide some talent,' said Hope.

'What do you mean?' Macleod asked.

'Strip the Willow. Who would have thought you would have done Strip the Willow? You nearly threw me off that back wall.'

'Nonsense,' said Macleod, and it was. When they'd come to the part where you swung round with each other, he felt he was the one being swung, not the other way around. Strip the Willow, a traditional Scottish ceilidh dance involved changing partners so often that Macleod felt dizzy by the end. Jane had dragged him out there with a smile and she was still smiling, and that's why Macleod was here. He was no dancer. This was not him, but he needed to give her the time and the space to enjoy herself.

Jane was looking resplendent. She had bought a new dress and even bought him a new suit. It was bright for his liking, but he would not complain and he had stood for a part of the night, watching his partner talk to so many people. Jane was vivacious. She could engage and then every now and again, he saw the head turn round to look for him, check to see what he was doing.

Someone walked past and suddenly Macleod had a baby on his knee. Well, it wasn't quite a baby, more like a toddler.

'Grumps, is it?' said Hope.

Macleod looked at her, giving a dark stare, but inside, he was loving it. 'You know I don't like it when Ross calls me that. And it's Gramps!'

'Well, he's got none of his own. Child needs some sort of grandparents. Even a Grumps and a Grandma. I don't see why you and Jane can't do it,' said Hope.

'He could have chosen you.'

'I am not old enough to be a grandparent,' said Hope. 'Oi, less of that,' she said at Macleod's raising of his eyebrows.

She swung her legs around to sit at right angles to the seat. Hope was wearing a dress, something Macleod didn't see often. It really suited her because she had a terrific figure. Yes, she was tall and yes, she was strong, but the dress, simply cut in a plain orange colour, looked perfect on her. She shone in a way he never had. Sassy. He laughed. One thing Macleod never was—sassy, or even sexy.

Macleod felt a hand reach up and touch his cheek. The child on his lap reaching up, tweaking his ears.

'Get off,' said Macleod. 'Grumps don't like.'

'See, you just said Grumps.'

'Enough,' said Macleod. He smiled and started bouncing the child on his knee. Angus, Ross's partner, suddenly came past.

'Do you mind if I grab him for a photograph?' he said to Macleod.

He offered the child straight away. The music had become slower. Some sort of waltz, Macleod reckoned. Then he realised that Hope had stood up. She reached down with her hand.

'I want to talk to you,' she said. 'Come and dance.'

Jane appeared at Macleod's side. 'Do you want this one?' she asked.

13

'If you want,' said Macleod. 'But Hope's just asked.'

He saw Jane looking at Hope's face. Then his woman half smiled. 'Go dance with your inspector,' said Jane. 'I'll be over there. Some top canapes.'

Macleod took to the floor with Hope, unsure at first quite where to put his hands when they danced. One minute they were quite close, then he tried to step back.

'Just put an arm up on my shoulder, an arm around the back of my waist, and don't be afraid to be close.'

'You realise you are much taller than me? I mean, I don't feel like a man dancing with a woman here. I feel like a child being pulled into his mother's . . .'

'Stop,' said Hope. She moved back and forward in time with the waltz, and Macleod tried to follow.

'Never come up with images again,' said Hope. 'We're just two colleagues. We're having a dance and we're up here because I want to talk to you quietly.'

'What about?' asked Macleod.

'Have you asked her?'

'I've tried,' he said. 'I can't get near her.'

'Well, she's a bride on her wedding day, to be fair. I doubt she's running away from you.'

'She's running,' said Macleod. 'I'm not sure that she's ready. Though you're right; she is doing well.'

Macleod saw Clarissa over his shoulder dancing with her husband, a broad smile across her face.

'The team's not the same without her,' said Hope. 'We're down Patterson. We could do with her back. We still haven't . . .'

'I know we haven't. We haven't found them yet. We haven't been able to get into the group. Ross said there would be more.

There will be more. It's coming.' Macleod bowed his head slightly, but found his chin being lifted by Hope.

'It wasn't your fault. We stopped two of them.'

'We nearly lost the lot, though.'

'But we didn't. Patterson will be okay, and Clarissa . . .'

'Clarissa will what? Be okay? I need her back in the unit, but I look at her now and I think, why? How can I do that? She doesn't deal with the horror as well as we do.'

'You deal with the horror?'

'Yes,' said Macleod. 'I deal with it. I process it. I get rid of it. Don't you?'

'I have cried myself to sleep at nights,' said Hope. 'Ask John. I've spent nights in his arms sometimes when things come back at me. Don't forget Cunningham had it rough, too.'

'I know, but I need Clarissa back. She's good for Ross as well. He's different.'

'Of course, he's different, Seoras. We all are. We've all struggled with this one. It's just you and I have had this before. Ross, too. Clarissa, she's not used to it in the same way. I mean, to have to hold on to your partner, to have to keep him alive.'

Their heads went down, and the pair danced together until the music stopped. There was a quick silence, a round of applause for the band, and then murmuring started.

'Are you okay, Seoras?' asked Hope.

'No,' he said. 'Neither are you. We need to end this, need to find them. The team needs to be put back the way it was. We need to . . .'

Suddenly, he was pulled very close, Hope hugging him tightly. 'Quiet,' she said, 'You need to talk to her. It's her big day, but we need to know. Do it.'

Macleod turned away from Hope, saw Clarissa with a glass

of champagne in her hand, and strode over to her.

'Congratulations,' he said. 'You look happy.'

'I am, Seoras. I really am. How are you?' Macleod went to speak, but no words came out.

'That's part of the problem,' she said, 'when it gets you like that. You haven't been able to leave it, have you? You haven't been able to deal with the fact that they got away, that they escaped. That's just the way it went. Sometimes it happens.'

'No,' said Macleod, 'that's not just the way it happens. Sometimes you need to get them because more are coming. We took an enormous hit.'

'Yes, we did.'

'But Patterson's going to be okay. He's sorry he is not here today, but it's just the way he's feeling.'

'I hope he's okay, and Susan, and I think I'm okay.'

'You've obviously landed on your feet. Ross is . . .'

'Ross has changed,' said Clarissa. 'Ross has become hardened. Something's going on in there.'

'Aye,' said Macleod. There was a silence.

Clarissa tapped Macleod on the shoulder. 'Tell me what it is. I've been avoiding you, but now you've got me. Tell me what it is.'

'I can't,' said Macleod.

'Tell me. Just come out with it and tell me.'

'We need you back,' he said. 'I know what you've seen has been horrific. I know what's happened, but you got through it. You succeeded. You did what you needed to do. It's not the same team without you. I need my bullish sergeant. I need my . . .'

'Rottweiler?' she said.

'Yes, my Rottweiler. When you come back—if you come

16

back—we need to get them. We need to.'

Macleod's phone vibrated. Instinctively, he reached for it, taking it out of his pocket before he even realised he had done it in such a rude fashion. It was a call from the duty sergeant at the station. He knew where they were. He wouldn't have called unless it was urgent. There came a tap on his shoulder. He turned and saw Hope mouthing the words, 'Lot's dead.'

Macleod held a hand up to Clarissa. 'Excuse me,' he said.

He made off a small distance before calling the sergeant. A minute later, he walked over to Jane, apologising, saying he had to go and pointing her toward Clarissa.

Four detectives headed off immediately from the wedding to get to the crime scene. But one remained, happy in her wedding dress, talking civilly to Jane. On the outside, Clarissa tried to smile as she spoke, but on the inside, she was feeling a panic.

Chapter 03

The Cairngorms looked stunning as the evening sun worked its way behind the mountains. The heathers spread across them showed up with the light, purple as the thistles were in flower. That, combined with the immature heather, cast a stunning carpet across the mountain's contours.

As the car drove into the car park of the Holy Glen Hotel, Macleod could see many ambulances, and police officers trying to herd people towards the other services. Outside on the road, he had seen coastguards on traffic duty. Such was the size of the operation, and he wondered what was going to face him. The desk Sergeant had talked about some kind of organised killing, almost medieval in the way it was carried out. The car pulled up, Ross driving, and Macleod stepped out to an acknowledgment from one of the uniformed sergeants on the scene.

'Detective Chief Inspector,' he said.

'So, how are we doing?' asked Macleod.

'Well, the area's sealed off. Forensics are about to go in. It's a mess though. I got people wandering around, stunned and in a mess. Been trying to get help to them all, and get a headcount. We've got as many ambulances as we can, but we're trying to get information from people with severe trauma. What they've seen has been . . .'

'What did they see?'

'Five people put to the gallows and killed. Prior to that, several people executed for not obeying instruction. Apparently, it's all been filmed.'

'Are we getting any descriptions of the attackers?'

'Well, they seem to have been disguised. I'm trying to round everything up for you, sir. Get you a better briefing. Maybe you want to check the scene first with forensics.'

Macleod was joined by Hope. Also arriving in the second car was Susan Cunningham. Macleod and Hope then walked over to the forensic wagon that had pulled up, donned sets of coveralls and then entered the front lobby of the Holy Glen Hotel.

The main lobby was looking distressed. Macleod could see the odd table having been turned over, glasses knocked to one side. Presumably, there'd been some sort of melee to get out. As he entered, he saw the figure of an Asian woman barking orders at people.

'Can you give me a minute?' she said, seeing Macleod. He nodded back.

Macleod stood for a moment with Hope looking around. 'What do you feel?' he asked.

'Fear. Genuine fear amongst the survivors.'

It took a moment before he was called forward by Jona and, as Macleod entered the conference room, he saw five corpses swinging.

'You got to us quick,' said Jona. 'I'll have those bodies down shortly. We're just taking the last of the photographs, checking through a few things. There are also some bodies on the floor.'

'Do you want to walk me through your initial thoughts?'

'Well, the initials are quite simple,' said Jona. 'A large group of people in here. You got one dead on the floor over there, one there, one there, and another there. All shot in the head, quick, accurate. Done by people that knew what they were doing. Although, given the distance some of them were shot at, possibly not specialists. More like people who've been trained recently. Not with practiced ease, shall we say?'

'Interesting,' said Macleod. 'What about the people on the gallows?'

'Still got to identify them. You can check with the duty sergeant out there. He might have a better idea. When we get them down, we'll be able to pull out some ID. Although, I think many people knew who these people were. There was a conference that was running, so there'll be a list.'

'White tuxedo on that one,' said Macleod.

'A little more ostentatious than some people I've seen out there,' said Hope. 'Maybe that's the boss boss.'

'You mean the big boss?' asked Jona. 'Like Seoras here?'

'Whatever. He's a dead boss,' said Macleod, ignoring the jibe. 'That woman on the end, she's like . . .'

'I would say she's in her nineties,' said Jona.

'Who hangs a ninety-year-old woman?' asked Macleod.

'Someone with a heck of a grievance. This has been filmed though. They said so outside. Done with that equipment over there. It's still on it what happened.'

'Well, that's a relief,' said Macleod. 'At least we've got that.'

'Nope. Sent to the cloud straight away. I suggest Ross gets involved in trying to find that account before it shuts. Well, it's probably shut already.'

'What do you mean?' asked Macleod.

'I mean, as that thing's filming, it's already firing it up into the glorious network above us. Wouldn't surprise me if it's out on all the usual channels.'

'Any similarities to previous?'

'Not that I'm aware of, but I haven't seen the film.'

'Hope, get me the duty Sergeant, then. I want somebody to come in here and talk me through what statements have been given. What people have been saying.'

She ran off, and Macleod turned back to Jona.

'Lovely wedding, wasn't it?' she said. 'She looked happy. Anything on when she's . . .'

'I was asking her when this happened. Bad timing.' Macleod stood and looked around for a moment. There was blood across tables. White tablecloths that were smeared with wine and blood and bits of—well, he didn't want to think about it.

'How many dead in total?' asked Macleod.

'I've got nine.'

He stared at the camera; he glared at the gallows. *Swept in,* he thought. *Swept in and just dispensed justice, but no kidnapping. Why not a kidnapping? Why wouldn't you kidnap this time if this is the same people? This is not what they did last time, but we found them last time, didn't we? This is a quicker way to do it. Maybe it's easier. Maybe it's . . .*

'You can come back to the real world, Seoras. I've got the sergeant here.'

'Sorry,' said Macleod, looking around him. 'I was just getting a feel. Speaking of which, Sergeant, can you tell us what you've been told so far? Does it add up?'

'We're still trying to pull the reports together, but from what the boys have been saying and from what we've been hearing, you've got the group come in. They're wearing grey monk's

21

habits, though they weren't at first. They seemed to have come in wearing jackets and hoodies, but these then come out as grey monk's habits. There's a stony face on the front, a metallic face.'

Macleod raised his eyes. Hope looked at him, but they both knew what they were thinking.

'They came in and told everybody to get on the ground. Sounds like they gave a count and then those who weren't down on their knees got shot. Four of them. Quite a dramatic way to get attention. I suspect that's those shot to the head, Jona.

'Then he made some sort of a speech. Mr Allen is apparently on the left-hand side there at the front. He's the guy who organised all this as the CEO of the overall company. They're saying that this group that gathered has organisations tied into it. An umbrella for companies. It's their big celebration. Someone said that there was a brother, a sister, a niece, somebody else's son, possibly, all swinging. Anyway, all related and somebody fingered that old woman as the worst.'

Macleod gave his head a bit of a shake. 'How? And how did they leave?'

'As far as I can gather, they just hanged these guys and then they packed up guns and went out the door.'

How did they get away? What did they get away in? What were they driving?

'Got the rest of the staff to interview as well. Look, Chief Inspector, we're absolutely maxed out here.'

'I'm not criticising,' said Macleod, 'but as quick as you can. If we get an idea of a vehicle, or whatever, we can still possibly trace.'

'Of course,' said the Sergeant. 'We'll get back on it.'

Macleod saw Susan Cunningham at the door dressed in a coverall suit and he pointed her out to Hope.

'She's calling for both of us,' said the Inspector. Together, the pair walked over. Susan Cunningham gave them a dour smile.

'That's the Allen Brothers corporation hanging up there. Just about everybody that's made it what it is.'

'How do you know that?'

'Talked to one owner of the hotel. Big corporation event. They've got names of everybody who was in attendance. Wasn't difficult picking out the top of the tree.'

'They were all staying here?' asked Macleod.

'Yes.'

'Get their rooms cordoned off? Probably worth you getting a few uniforms and get some searches going in the rooms. Not sure if it's going to yield anything but could do. If you see anything suspicious, make a stop and get forensics in.'

'Of course,' said Cunningham, and raced away.

'A bit of a long shot, though, isn't it?' said Hope.

'We have got very little at the moment and if this is who I think it is, we're going to need to be on form.'

'Okay,' said Hope. 'Point taken. What do we do now?'

'Well, we clear out of here and—oh, hang on a minute,' said Macleod, looking up. 'That corner. Small, aren't they?'

'You're talking about the security cameras.'

'Very subtle,' said Macleod. 'Very subtle.'

'What makes you think they didn't cut them, though?' asked Hope.

'They just filmed this. The killers uploaded the film for broadcast. They want us to know,' said Macleod. 'Where's Ross?'

Hope disappeared off and came back two minutes later.

'Follow me,' she said.

His Inspector took Macleod through the lobby over to some offices. She held the door open for Seoras, who walked in and saw Ross sitting beside several screens and a keyboard to operate the in-house surveillance.

'Looks like we have everything,' he said.

'Good,' said Macleod. He leaned back against the desk behind him. 'Let's see what happened.'

For the next couple of minutes, the trio sat and watched as events were played for them. Macleod jumped as the first number of shots went off, killing off those who didn't kneel quick enough. Macleod then shivered as he watched the cold, callous execution of the Allens. Maybe they weren't the best of people, but the ending was grim. Macleod stared as the men in the grey monk's habits disappeared and then got Ross to rewind it.

'Let's get some close-ups,' he said. 'See what we can discover.'

Ross ran through the film again, but this time he would zoom in on particular images. Grey monks, all with those steely grey masks on. Macleod became impatient as Ross fired the camera in to this section, and then that section, occasionally saving images.

'You're going to tell me none of them show the face?' said Macleod.

'It's the first time I've seen the images. I'm running through them. This is why you don't stand with me when I'm working.'

'Don't mind him,' said Hope. 'Boss is just desperate to get a lead out of this. We all are.'

'You think we're going to see anything different on the camera in the room than what we're seeing from here?' asked Macleod.

'I'll go through it,' said Ross. 'You never know what people are doing. Maybe they adjusted the mask. I might see something. Maybe I can start cross-referencing heights.'

'One thing is bothering me,' said Macleod to Hope. 'How many of them are there?' 'They're rolling out large numbers of people. The organisation of this, it's good. Timing, everything is slick. The place they've attacked. Perfect. It's far enough out of the way that you won't be disturbed. If someone calls the police or whatever, it's going to take time to get here. You have time to get clear. You have time not to blow it.'

Macleod looked back to the screen in front of him and saw that Ross was blowing up a section. The picture in front of him showed a grey mask with a hood around it. The darkness inside meant Macleod couldn't see what colour of hair the man had. It was clearly a man, for the shoulders were big, the stature wrong for a woman.

Macleod stared at the screen. A pair of piercing eyes were looking back at him. Possibly brown, possibly green. He wasn't sure, but they stared. Macleod for a moment was filled with a fistful of malice.

'That's the leader,' he said. 'That's the one that was talking. Listen up,' said Macleod. 'We're going to get this guy this time.'

'You're saying these are the same people?'

'I know it,' said Macleod, his fist suddenly shaking. 'It's going to take an effort, but we're going to get him this time. That psychopath has just casually killed nine people. What are you up to this time?' asked Macleod, to the mask on the screen. 'What's the gameplay?'

Macleod sat down. He was feeling tired after the day's festivities, but he knew he'd have a long shift through the night. 'We'll get you this time. We'll get you.'

25

Chapter 04

With parts of the Holy Glen Hotel now having been swept, Macleod could set up several rooms for interviews. They had the local staff to get through, as well as the guests, and many were in a state of confusion and terror. Because of the sheer number, Macleod had organised teams of interviewers to sift through and find out who knew what, building upon the basic work that the uniformed officers had already done. And those who had been closest to the action, or who may have the most evidence to give, were passed on to Macleod and Hope. The hotel manager, Angela MacIver, was deeply upset as she sat across from Macleod.

'They've got some of my people,' she said. 'We did a head count afterwards. At first, it was, well, it was chaos. I mean, your officers thought people were running here and there, but some had just been threatened with a gun, some had seen people die. It was a mess, an absolute mess. You couldn't expect people to, well, follow procedures with all that going on.'

Macleod wasn't sure how many hotels would have a proce-dure for an execution-style incursion such as this. Certainly, it was unexpected, and he was quite grateful for all that the hotel manager had achieved since the officers had arrived on scene.

'How many have they got?' asked Macleod.

'At least seven. From what I understand, the keys that they used to get in—because you need keys to come in through that door as it's not one that guests would use—they were taken off the main housekeeper. She's still missing, but the access they used on the touch system, the key card was hers. A few others were also activated, one of the concierge cards, another handyman, but we've got six missing. I gave the names to the sergeant I spoke to earlier.'

'We are trying to get them back,' said Macleod. 'This may be a unit that's worked before. In those cases, so-called parties that weren't guilty in their opinion were returned unharmed. I'm hoping that's going to be the case, but I can't guarantee it.'

'You think it's those minister murders?'

'It's unconfirmed. There are a couple of theories.'

'Everyone said they were wearing masks. That was the case in that other set of killings, wasn't it? They were on the telly with the masks, but they didn't do what they did here.'

Macleod could see the woman's shoulders shake. Her head shuddered before a tip forward, and her hands flew to it. Tears flowed. He thought they were from shock as much as anything else.

'We can't say if it's the same people,' said Hope, 'but we'll do our best to get them back. You've been very helpful. I'd suggest that you try and comfort your staff at the moment. Give them what help you can.'

'Had nothing like this,' she blurted, the manager lifting her head. 'Never, in all my time running hotels. The owner's coming. He's just a mess. What do you do? How do you get

27

back after this?'

'You clean up and you try to get back to normality.'

'We've got bookings tumbling already,' said Angela.

'You have, of course, changed all keys and codes?' asked Hope.

'Straightaway, straightaway after, in case they came back. It's protocol, but then the guests were locked out and we had to open all the doors for you. We gave your officers one keycard.'

'That's much appreciated,' said Macleod. 'Go to your staff now. If we have anything else, we'll speak further.'

As the woman left the room escorted by a female constable, Macleod turned to Hope. 'It is the same people, isn't it? But this is a step up. This is . . .'

'Is it revenge for what we did last time? We thwarted them at the end of the day.'

'We thwarted them?' queried Macleod. 'I wouldn't have gone that far. It's been worrying me. These last couple of months—it's been worrying me.'

He stood up and walked to the window of the room, pulling back the curtains. The Cairngorms were being lost in the fading light in the almost toffee glow settling over them, but its beauty was lost to Macleod. Instead, his eyes saw nothing while his mind raced.

'We need to keep this quiet, the footage in particular.'

'Not going to be easy, Seoras, with that many people having seen it. People are dead too, execution style.'

'No,' said Macleod loudly.

'What?' asked Hope.

'It's the main core of the press arriving, all the vans outside.'

'We got the cordon up, though. They're all well back.'

'They're all well back. Of course, they are, but they'll get to someone. It'll be out: execution style.'

'You want me to deal with them?'

'No,' said Macleod, 'Let them wait. We need to get closer to understanding how the killers got away, how they arrived.'

'Ross said that several vans arrived, black like before, or at least three of them. They then drove away. Jona's working on the tyre marks, but they're tyre tracks like every other one of those vans. Wherever they're being acquired from, they've been acquired legally,' said Hope. 'We'll need to get a clean van to trace through properly. They've been very thorough, always efficient.'

There was a rap at the door.

'Come in,' said Macleod, and saw his newest detective enter the room. Susan Cunningham wasn't quite Hope's six feet. She was similar in her demeanour, except where Hope would sport her leather jacket, Cunningham might wear a tight sports jacket. Same jeans and boots worn underneath, though.

'Seoras, I found a little boy. I think he may have seen something. Would you come into the interview room down the corridor?'

Macleod looked over at Hope. 'You might be better,' he said to her. 'Friendlier face rather than this old guy.'

'Susan's there with you. Let her run it. You'll be fine.'

Macleod was less worried about how he would talk to the child and more concerned with stepping in front of Hope. Hope was the DI. He ideally wanted her to run the case, but he would give her a view from above. Now, with so few of them, Macleod was having to step down and take charge.

Susan Cunningham led Macleod down the corridor and into another room. There were several laundry bales in the far corner and a makeshift desk had been put up behind which sat a small child. A liaison officer was sitting with him.

'Timmy,' said Susan. A little boy looked up. He had short brown hair, cut in a bowl shape, and was wearing a shirt and tie.

'Where's his parents?' asked Macleod in a whisper.

'They got trampled on in the stampede, both gone to hospital. Nothing serious.'

Macleod nodded and sat down in front of the child. The kid looked up at him wide-eyed and looking quite afraid.

'Timmy,' said Macleod, 'I am Detective Chief Inspector Macleod, but you can call me Seoras.' He looked at the child, grinning. 'Yes. It's a bit of a different name,' he said, 'Gaelic, but that doesn't matter. Susan here says that you saw people in the van.'

The child dropped his head back down to the table.

'It's okay,' said Macleod, 'I just need to know anything you can tell me about it.'

The child must have been seven or eight and his eyes looked so sullen when he next raised his head.

'They weren't nice people,' said Timmy suddenly. 'They pushed people into the vans. The people were scared and screaming. They were yelling. I had my phone. I was taking photographs of some spiders in the stones.'

'Where?' asked Macleod.

'Outside. I had been sitting with Mum and Dad. They'd been having a drink. They told me I could play just outside. Then, after I was taking the photographs, these people ran out. Banged into my parents.'

'You took them on your phone?' asked Macleod.

'Yes,' he said. 'I haven't had it that long.'

'Where is the phone?'

30

'It's on me.'

'Can you show me the phone?' asked Macleod, 'and can you show me the photographs? I'm rubbish with phones. I can't use them. Susan will tell you; I don't know what I'm doing with them.'

Macleod stood up and came around the table, indicating to the officer with Timmy, that she should make some space. Timmy nervously took his phone out and Macleod watched the child punch in a number code that seemed to comprise at least ten numbers. Macleod struggled to get through a code of six.

'Here,' said Timmy. Macleod looked at the photograph of an enormous spider across some stones. 'That's the one with the white back. It's interesting, isn't it?'

'Yes,' said Macleod, 'very interesting, but can you show me more of the photographs you took? Did you take any of the people running past?'

'I took some,' said Timmy. 'I don't think they're very good.'

'Well, can you show me?' asked Macleod.

The child fired his finger across the screen and quickly whipped through several photographs. Macleod saw masked men running past, and several pictures of the vans. They were indeed black, similar to the ones that had come before. No doubt the CCTV would confirm that, anyway. They probably would've used false number plates. Macleod didn't think there was much chance of catching a break from the van itself. Timmy continued to fire his finger across. The child must have taken the best part of twenty to twenty-five photographs.

'How did you get so many done so quick?' asked Macleod.

'You press the button, and it keeps taking,' said Timmy. Macleod looked at Cunningham. She gave him a face as if

31

everyone knew that. He decided not to say anything, but looked back down at the photographs Timmy was skimming through.

'Stop, please,' said Macleod. 'No, backwards.'

Timmy flicked his finger in the opposite direction. Macleod could see a masked man except the mask had slipped.

'Susan,' said Macleod, 'there's a partial shot here. I think there's a good half a face, almost. Don't know how pixelated it'll be, but we may get something from it.'

'He doesn't look very nice, does he?' said Timmy.

'No indeed, he doesn't. Detective Cunningham,' started Macleod and then checked himself. 'Susan's going to need to borrow your phone. We'll try to get it back to you as soon as we can. I'll maybe even get you a better one, as you may have caught one man who did this.'

'They did lots of big bangs and there was lots of screaming,' said Timmy.

'There was, but why didn't you run back to your parents, though?'

'I was taking photographs of the spiders. I stood over them. Didn't want anyone to stand on them.'

Macleod wondered at the innocence of the child, but he gave him a smile before turning to Cunningham. 'Susan, make sure we get copies of all those photographs. You're going to have to secure the phone, and then let's see if somebody can get Timmy up to see his parents in the hospital.'

'Are they okay? This lady said they were okay,' Timmy said, pointing towards the officer with him.

'She doesn't lie,' said Macleod. 'They have had a fright and a bit of a bashing, but your parents will be okay. Nothing nasty happened to them. They just got a bit injured. They'll be fine, but we'll see if we can get you up to the hospital.'

The child stood up and went to leave the room. Macleod tapped the officer on her shoulder.

'First, make sure the press doesn't get near him,' said Macleod. 'I think he has been through enough as it is.' He watched the child leave with the officer before giving Cunningham a smile. 'Good work. Get Ross on the facial recognition as well, see if we can pick up who it is. Finally, they made a slip. Looks like he was stumbling when that happened.'

'I'll be right on it,' said Cunningham. As she left the room, there was a knock on the door.

'You in here, Seoras?' asked a voice. It was calm. Macleod recognised it as Jona Nakamura. She marched in wearing her coverall suit, hood pulled down, black hair hanging out the back. In times of stress, she was always a pleasant face to see, but Macleod could see a glint in her eye. 'You can't tell me I've had two breaks in one day. Not this close together.'

'DNA,' she said. 'We've got some DNA of one of our friends.'

'From what?' asked Macleod.

'One of your officers interviewed one guest. Said that they saw one attacker put a hand down where a glass had been broken. Cut him. Said that the blood was from the attacker. It was small, not a lot. But we were able to get all the glass fragments, and I think I've got something. We'll go through the process, see what we can get, maybe a lead.'

'If he's been brought in for something before. Difficult though, could be nothing. They didn't use people that were criminals before.'

'DNA,' said Jona, grinning. 'We got a chance. Don't poo-poo it before it's been checked. You're due a couple of breaks. The last one didn't go so well.'

'Don't you start. That's all the press will be saying. But top priority, please—get that DNA checked and get back to me.'

'Already on its way,' she said. 'Have we got any catering coming here? I don't think the kitchens are going to do anything.'

'Tell the sergeant at the front coordinating the scene. We could probably do with a run through for everyone.'

Jona gave a nod and left the room, leaving Macleod on his own. With no one looking, he clenched his right fist and gave a little pump of it. *Two possibilities in one day, two chances. What were the odds? Things were going his way. After the last time when nothing fell, nothing could pin people down. This time, things were moving.*

Chapter 05

Macleod snatched a phone call to his partner Jane at around about seven o'clock in the morning. He'd been up all night along with the rest of the team, and many of the officers were flagging when the arrival of breakfast buoyed him. An officer had been dispatched and brought back many bacon, sausage, and egg rolls from a nearby town. That was the thing about uniform. They always had a way of knowing what was about, where they could go to get something at whatever hour of the day. Worth their weight in gold, they were.

Macleod sat with his little plastic box open and a bacon, sausage, and fried egg looking at him from inside a roll. Biting into it, he felt the yellow liquid from the egg roll down the outside of his cheeks. He quickly reached with his free hand, wiping it before it would fall onto the suit he was wearing. He was due to do a press conference in half an hour, and the last thing he needed was for stains to be down the front of his clothing.

That was the crazy thing. You'd been up all night, and you were still expected to look pristine. Ross had departed the scene in the middle of the night, heading back to the office to run through image recognition with his computers. He and his female detectives were still there to guide what was going on. Hope had spent most of the night coordinating with the sergeant about who could go home and who couldn't. A separate team had been formed and were scouring the country, trying to work out where the hotel's kidnapped workers had been taken.

'You watch that egg,' said Hope, approaching Macleod. She had a bacon roll in her mouth, and her words were slightly muffled.

'Yes, mum,' he said. He noticed Hope was holding a separate container in her other hand.

'How come you get two?'

'That's not for me; that's Jona's.'

'How come you look after her and not your boss?' said Macleod, teasing.

'She always forgets. She gets herself worked up, constantly charging around, and her team isn't the same as us.'

'What, they don't live off their bellies?' said Macleod, laughing again. He glanced over at Susan Cunningham, who was shoving a roll in her own mouth. 'That's why you're on the team,' he said. 'You've got a hearty appetite.' She looked at him, not sure how to take the comment, and Hope burst out laughing.

'He's joking,' said Hope.

'Anyway, where is she?'

'Somewhere over there,' spat Susan Cunningham through the food in her mouth. She then raised a finger, pointing towards the edge of the hotel. A white coverall suit with some black hair bobbing up and down seemed to approach quickly.

'She must be hungry,' said Macleod.

'Chief Inspector,' shouted Jona from a distance. 'Chief Inspector.'

Macleod put down his roll. She was out in public, and she was shouting Chief Inspector. This must be serious.

'What is it, Jona?'

She came sprinting up, completely ignoring Hope, and running straight to Macleod, a piece of paper in her hand.

'We've got a match. DNA match. It's an Andrew Taybrite. Apparently, he's a banker in Edinburgh. Just sent the detail off to Ross. He's in our system. Pulled in for some minor theft when he was younger. Last known address is Edinburgh.'

Macleod pulled the piece of paper from her and stared at the image of the man. He looked as if he was in his thirties, and the image was the standard dire-looking one that everyone gave when having their photograph taken by the police. He picked up his phone and called the Edinburgh police, working his way through to one of the Chief Inspectors that he knew there.

'Andrea,' he said, 'Seoras.'

'Bet you've been up all night. I saw on the news. It's . . .'

'It's awful. Listen, I've got a lead. I need you to act on it for me. I'm going to send you some details of an Andrew Taybrite, banker working out of Edinburgh. Got his DNA here. We believe he may have been involved. Need you to apprehend and then bring him in, and I'll be down for questioning.'

'Of course, I'll get a squad ready. Is he violent?'

'They arrived here, executed some people, and shot other people in the head. I'd say he was violent,' said Macleod. 'Be careful. I'd send an armed unit to get him.'

'That's understood. Get the detail down to us. It'll take me twenty minutes, half an hour, to assemble the squad. Then will get straight on it.'

'No one knows about this except my people and your people. I will not make it public until you have him. We keep everything quiet. If you can, pick him up quietly. No fuss, no nonsense, but be careful.'

'I appreciate what you're saying. I'll do my best.'

'We believe this may be the same group,' said Macleod, 'as before with the ministers. That's what I mean. Be careful.'

'Will do.'

Macleod was like a small child knowing that a lollipop was coming, but the bearer of the gift just hadn't quite arrived yet. Almost jumping up and down, his glee at being able to get one of these people was obvious. At last, a way into their heavily protected clique.

He spent the next half an hour going through reports, talking to Hope, and walking about the scene to give himself something to do. He was excited, very excited, but he couldn't show it. Too many TV cameras out front, and he knew they would zoom in on him. He was talking to the sergeant covering the scene when his phone went off. It had been an hour since he'd called Edinburgh. Andrea spoke to him quickly.

'Seoras, we went to the address. He's not there at the moment. We spoke to a neighbour who said he'd gone to the Cairngorms. Gave us an address.'

'I'm in the Cairngorms,' said Macleod. 'Send it up to me. We'll get onto it. Look, thanks, Andrea, much appreciated.'

'Of course,' she said. 'Good luck.'

Macleod called the Inverness station, requesting backup in the form of an armed unit. The address that Andrea sent him led to a small lodge sat up in the hills away from the road. It would take him a good half an hour to reach it, and he set off with Hope, leaving Cunningham to look after the scene.

They rendezvoused with an armed unit from Inverness some ten minutes from the house in a layby. There were no markings on any of the cars, and Macleod held back, allowing the vehicles of the armed unit to move ahead.

They approached a small driveway up to a cottage that was surrounded by trees. You could barely see it from the main road, but having taken the smaller C class road towards it, they turned into the driveway, parking their three cars. There was another car sitting there. Smoke came from the chimney of the house.

The leader of the armed unit came towards Macleod. 'Someone's in,' he said. 'Are you happy?'

'Find out who's in there. Bring them out, but be careful,' said Macleod.

He stood well back with Hope, watching the team in front of him operate. They surrounded the house, and then, using a large megaphone, they announced the police were here. Advising they were armed, he asked for whoever was inside to come out. A voice called from inside.

'Don't come any closer.' A Scottish accent. It was harsh and gruff. 'Don't come closer. I will execute this man. Andrew Taybrite is his name.'

Execute him? thought Macleod. *Who, why, and how would they get away? The house was surrounded.*

'Come out now,' said the firearms officer.

'We're going to execute him. He has failed in his duty. He has failed us.'

Through a radio set, the leader of the operation asked Macleod how likely it was they would execute the man.

'They've just killed five people by execution at the hotel I was at previously. They also killed people before that for not getting down on their knees quick enough. I would say it's highly likely if they think they've been compromised, but I don't understand how they'll escape.'

'If that's the case, then we will go in. We'll surround quickly. We'll get up close, and then we'll make sure that we bring out Mr Taybrite alive. Can't guarantee anyone else.'

'Your call,' said Macleod. 'You know what to do here. Not me.'

There was an affirmative over the radio. Macleod eagerly watched the house. The team manoeuvred around it, peering in windows. He saw hand signals, and then a small battering ram being brought up towards the front door.

'I've never seen something like this,' said Hope, 'but I don't understand something.'

'How are they going to get away?' murmured Macleod. 'You'd have to have something like a trapdoor somewhere else down to a tunnel to run out, but that's asking a lot.'

'Stay back,' came a voice from inside the house. 'Stay back.'

Macleod listened. Something wasn't right.

'Stay back, stay back.' It repeated the message. Macleod listened again intently now. 'Stay back,' said the voice a third time. He could see the small battering ram being readied, about to be driven into the front door. Around the house, men were ready to race in with guns armed. 'I said stay back,' spoke the voice.

There was a crackle in it. *A crackle*, thought Macleod, *almost like an over loudness. Not like when somebody shouted, and their voice failed. More like when the connection on a microphone was slightly dodgy.*

'No,' shouted Macleod. 'No,' his hands waving furiously. He

went to run from behind the car but saw the battering ram being driven into the front door. The world went crazy.

Something exploded inside the house. Glass flew everywhere, and the man about to go in fell backwards to the floor. Macleod was knocked off his feet by the blast, although it wasn't enough to knock Hope over. Glass rained down all around him, and he covered his head.

There were screams from ahead. People yelling. Getting to his knees, he saw those on the outer perimeter of the armed team running in, stepping past those on the floor. Was this a way of protecting? He wasn't sure but saw others pulling some back. He heard voices talking about rooms being clear, other rooms being searched. By the time Hope had picked him up and he walked towards the main building, he saw people coming out.

Macleod picked up his phone and called the station, demanding ambulances and assistance to the address. He raced forward, and one officer put his hand up, took away his mask and shouted at Macleod.

'We're clear in there. There's nobody in there. At least nobody alive.'

'What do you mean?' asked Macleod. Macleod went to run forward, but the man pushed him back.

'We've pulled everyone back,' he said. 'Just had a bomb go off in our face and I don't want another one. We step back.' Macleod watched as armed officers were being pulled away. People screaming.

'I've called for the ambulance. I've called for everyone.'

'Good,' said the man and ran towards the car, pulling out first aid kits. Macleod looked to his left. One man had his jacket ripped open. Someone was working on his chest. The

41

man who had led the team was lying on the floor, motionless.

'What about him?' asked Macleod.

One man doing compressions on someone else simply shook his head.

'He's gone.'

Macleod was suddenly cold. He watched Hope race past him, helping to treat someone, patching up their arm as best she could. She was working hard, but Macleod was struggling to comprehend.

They'd got DNA. They'd got the jump on the group, and yet they were already with Taybrite. Was he in there? Who was? What had happened?

It was ten minutes before Hope came to him, and Macleod was waiting by the car as the ambulances raced in.

'Seoras, are you okay? Seoras?'

Macleod was in shock. He couldn't think. 'Hi. What have we done?'

'Snap out of it,' he heard. 'Seoras, snap out of it. We need to think about this. We need to come up with a plan. A plan, Seoras, we need . . .'

But Hope's voice was distant. Macleod had never seen such a disaster. He had got hold of them. He had a way in, but now all he had was a dead colleague and many more injured.

Chapter 06

Macleod felt like the day dragged on him. Yes, it had kicked off with a bang, a deadly bang, and the mood around the site of the bomb was sombre, to say the least. What worried Macleod the most was that these killers seemed to be happy to include the police amongst those who should be meted out with justice. The sheer act of following them was punished.

Macleod had returned to the hotel to finish up interviews there. He also placed a call down to Andrea in Edinburgh to investigate Andrew Taybrite more deeply. He would've loved to have sent one of his people down, but Ross was still working hard on the facial recognition, running computer checks from his end. Hope was tied up with the hotel, ably assisted by Cunningham.

Macleod was missing a second sergeant. Missing a DC as well. The likelihood of Patterson being back soon was not good. Macleod thought he might have to reach out again, but the more significant situation was his missing Rottweiler. Clarissa would've been the one he'd have sent down to Edinburgh. In and amongst those financial institutions, she would know how to play it.

There was a style about Macleod that didn't fit at times. He wasn't the cleverest academically, though he could sniff out a killer from anywhere. Clarissa, for all her hard-nose tactics, was educated, mixed in the classier world. Macleod was a man of the streets, and the snobbery and the flashing of money riled him, but it also affected his judgment.

He hadn't phoned her either. He hadn't had time. Surely Jane had. Of course, she would know, though. Clarissa would have seen it on the news. It's just typical though, four months with nothing major, and on the evening of her wedding, everything kicked off right when he wanted to talk to her. Right when he wanted to . . . Well, maybe that had been a bad idea as well. She would've been happy, though. He wanted to talk to her when she was happy.

Though she was happy at her wedding, the past still haunted her. Only two days before, her husband-to-be had commented to Macleod how she still cried, still woke up fretful about Patterson. The man was going to be okay. The man would certainly live a life and one that could be full. Whether he returned to police work, time would tell.

Macleod had returned from the hotel on his own, leaving Hope behind. She could cover off any new information. Besides, Jona was now up at the blown-out building, digging through the remains, preventing anyone from going in. Now, in the middle of the night and with no sleep in maybe the last thirty-six hours—or was it forty-eight—Macleod would have time to look inside. He was already waiting in his coverall when she approached.

'You took your time,' he said.

'Forensics takes time. You know that. Don't have a go at me just because you're desperate to get in here. You got caught out. We got caught out. And they hurt us bad, Seoras. Don't come on to other people with an attitude like that.'

'Of course not,' he muttered.

'It's just, you blame yourself. Well, it wasn't your fault. They set the trap. They blew our man to kingdom come.'

'What did you find inside?' asked Macleod.

'Come with me,' said Jona.

She led the chief inspector in through the front door of the building. Not that there was much of it left. Inside was a mess, ripped apart when the bomb had gone off. He saw a sofa on one side burnt to a crisp, but the most horrific scene was the man sitting on a chair, but with his feet in the air, the chair having tipped backwards. It landed on its back, and the head had snapped and rolled to one side.

'That's Andrew Taybrite,' said Jona. 'I've been speaking with the fire service and calling in a few favours from the military. This was activated from outside. I'm still working on the exact composition of the bomb. Maybe we can trace something that way, but there was no one else in here. Also, Andrew Taybrite was dead beforehand.'

'They knew we were coming.'

'Very much,' said Jona. 'Whether they made him leave his DNA there or whether he screwed up and this is their punishment for it, I don't know. But they would've realised that we had his DNA. If he was working with them . . .'

'If he was working with them,' repeated Macleod, 'then he would've been up here, anyway. He would've told people this is where he was going. They would've known that about him, and they came and put him here and set him up as a trap. We would've gone after him. This is his punishment.'

'It is a bit of a change for them, though, isn't it?'

'Only if it is a punishment,' said Macleod. 'The other one,

our other witness, previously jumped out of the window of a hospital. This group's tight-knit. Either that or it's . . .'

'All right. Certainly, there's a tight rein on people. Can drive them to do things like this, but as I was saying, the bomb activated from elsewhere. They were watching. I can't find anything that would've tripped the bomb. They would have had eyes on the place.'

'I'll send people out to scout around, see if they've left anything, but the way they operate, I'm not so sure.' Macleod looked around the inside shell of the building. He noted the blackened wallpaper. He saw a part where the ceiling had fallen in.

'If you're going to do this, Jona, you'd have to have a bit of expertise, wouldn't you?'

'If I set something like this up, yes. Seoras, somebody in the group has worked with bombs before, whether that's military or a former terrorist. They've got somebody in. I'll try to see if there's a signature to it, but currently, I can't tell. The man over there,' she turned and pointed to a man in Army fatigues, 'he might tell me. As soon as he lets me know, I'll let you know.'

'Okay, thanks,' said Macleod, turning away. 'I'm not sure it was worth the wait.'

'One more thing,' said Jona. Macleod turned back and looked at her. Her eyes were incredibly serious. More than normal.

'What is it, Jona?'

'We found a cylinder on the floor. We think from the explosion that it may have been sitting behind Andrew Taybrite when he toppled over. Except the explosion would've thrown it off that wall. I reckon it ricocheted and landed over here.'

'Close to the bomb then,' said Macleod.

'Yes, except that it's a special cylinder, bombproof by the

looks of it. It would've stayed intact. There's no reason for it to be in here. Except . . .'

'Except it was left,' said Macleod. 'Did you open it?'

'It took us a while, because we had to check it, but we have. I've got the contents out in my van. Come with me.'

The pair walked out of the building and Macleod found the fresh air outside to be a boon. Inside, everything was charred, choking, as if thick smoke was still lingering on in some invisible way. Outside wasn't exactly pine fresh, but the wind had dispersed the smell. There was a background residual, a heavy residual, but it wasn't assaulting your nose like inside.

Jona entered her wagon from the rear and Macleod followed and saw a small clear plastic bag. Some details were written out on a piece of paper. Beside it in another plastic bag was an envelope.

'The letter came in that,' said Jona. 'We fished it out delicately. I've scanned it for fingerprints. There's none. You'll see that the writing's a bit of a mess. We think it's done left-handed. We'll get it to an expert, but the group's doing their usual, covering tracks. Maybe they even got somebody random in the group to do it. I doubt we're going to have a chance of matching it with anything, because we don't even know where to begin.'

'Okay,' said Macleod. 'You don't give me a face like that because somebody's left a note and we can't connect with whoever's written it.'

'No. Look at what it says.'

Macleod stared at the letter.

You were too close last time. Look what happened. DCI Macleod, stay off our trail. Otherwise, there'll be family consequences.

47

'Family consequences,' said Macleod out loud.

'That's a direct threat,' said Jona. 'Maybe you should . . .'

'We take precautions,' said Macleod. 'Don't forget, Jane's had the experience of certain people.'

He remembered back to when a former forensic officer of his had been put on a cross, diverting him away while his own wife had been attacked. A man seeking to dump her into an acid bath. Hope had saved her. Hope had paid with a scar that she still bore across her cheek.

'There's a low level of security now. I want to keep it that way,' said Macleod. 'Jane gets worried otherwise.'

'With good reason,' said Jona. 'Just take care. They seem to be stepping up the game. It's all got a little more deadly.'

'It has. I'm going to head back to the hotel,' he said. 'I need to inform Hope about this. You come up with anything else?'

'You'll be the first to know,' said Jona. 'They made a mistake, though. There is hope.'

Macleod smiled. 'They made two mistakes. Hopefully, Ross will have something on the other one soon.'

Macleod drove back in the car, trundling through the Cairngorms in the middle of the night. His headlights swept across the road. As he turned around the tree-lined corners, he wondered if he saw someone lurking in the darkness. He wasn't prone to worries, but now, as Jona had said, everything seemed ramped up a little. *Family, though*, he thought. *He had Jane. Or did they mean something else? Did they mean his family in terms of who he worked with? The detective family.*

They'd already struck at Patterson. They'd scared off Clarissa. Macleod found his eyes drooping, and he rolled down the windows of the car. The fresh air hit him, shaking him awake until he reached the hotel. There were plenty of lights on inside and searches were still continuing. As he went to step into the hotel, his mobile rang. He looked down. It was Andrea from Edinburgh.

'You're working late,' he said to her.

'Aren't we all?' she said. 'Sorry to hear.'

'Thanks.' Macleod cut her off. 'It's been a bit of a day. Tell me you got something.'

'Andrew Taybrite, Banker by trade. Apparently, he's a bit of an activist in his time. Nothing definite. Wasn't one of the financial whizzes. He wasn't a person who was going to fly up the ranks. He did well, but he was very keen on it being all by the book. No risks, nothing that would be picked out as dodgy. In fact, he called out several traders. In fact, he's flagged several people up to authorities before. Not police, but on financial irregularities. To HMRC, people like that.'

'Any friends there who can tell us a bit more about him? Where he spent his weekends?'

'All we know is he went up to the Cairngorms. Used to have a partner. Split with her nine months ago. But he was rather vocal when the killings of the ministers happened. Apparently, had little good to say about them, actually justified what was happening. It was low level, though. They didn't suspect he was involved. In fact, he was sitting in the office when the first attack happened. If he's part of who you're chasing, it looks like it was a later decision.'

'A recruit. Maybe they've been recruiting. It's been four months,' said Macleod. 'We've been sat still. They haven't.'

'You don't know that, Seoras; you can't investigate what's not there. Stay the course. Don't beat yourself up. Stay the course. Make sure you follow everything up.'

'Thanks, Andrea,' he said. 'It helps to know we've got people behind us. Take care.'

'Take care, Seoras.' she said, 'You've lost one man too many already.'

Macleod nodded, although she was talking to him on the phone. He closed the call and thought about what he was going to say to Hope. He couldn't lose anyone else. It was time to go on the offensive. They needed to chase the leads. Needed to get hold of these people. They had killed nine people in this hotel and now they had killed someone else. The stakes were too high to be scared off.

Chapter 07

It was just before noon when Macleod made it back to the police station in Inverness. The day had turned grey, and a light drizzle was coming down, forcing him to turn up his collar in the short walk from his car to the rear door of the police station. As he'd approached in the car, he had seen several reporters pitching their stories outside the front of the station, and he was glad to have avoided them. He felt weary and the bags under his eyes were only getting bigger. Trudging up the stairs to his office on the top floor, Macleod was greeted by his secretary. Linda gave him a pained look.

'You really need sleep.'

Macleod waved his hand. 'I need coffee. Please.'

'It's on the desk. Saw you come in. I've held up all the routine paperwork for now. I take it that's for the best.'

'It will be held for a while,' said Macleod, 'as the Assistant Chief Constable will be looking for me.'

'He said he wants an update as soon as you can, also asking if you need any more help.'

Macleod nodded. 'Advise him I'll get back to him as soon as I can.'

He opened the door of his office. There was indeed a cup

of steaming coffee sitting on his desk. After taking off his coat and hanging it up, he plonked himself in his chair, but he couldn't sit there for long. He'd fall asleep if he remained. Macleod needed to see Ross, but he also needed to get his thoughts in order.

Although he didn't like to admit it, the note had shaken him. *Family consequences.* It was the lot of a police officer that occasionally you may get threatened, but Macleod had endured more than a fair share of it. Hope, the scar on her face, reminded him of that every day.

A number of people had commented to him how much of a pity it was. Of course, she was an attractive woman, and he guessed they thought a scar to the face somehow took away from her beauty. He believed it added to it. Otherwise, when you looked at her, you wouldn't have seen her courage, but there it was, displayed for all to see.

He stood up, took his cup, and looked out the window, cursing again that he was now up in this office, giving a completely different vista to the old one he had. He used to enjoy it. You could see people going about their daily business. Here, it was all cars.

Windows were good, he thought. Windows from an office, especially. He pondered on who would have the best office. Air traffic controllers, he thought. Especially the ones at the remote airports. You must be able to see for miles. Sea, hills, greenery. In terms of mental health, it must have been a great perk of the job, or maybe the other stresses made up for that.

He gave his head a shake. Macleod was tired. He was drifting. He sipped his coffee quickly, feeling the fatigue. Sleep was needed. At least, catch a couple of hours. He drank the rest of the coffee, put the cup on the desk, marched to his door, opening it to his secretary outside.

'Can you set the camp bed up for me, Linda? I need to go down and see Ross, and then it's Fort Knox after that.'

He saw his secretary grin. Fort Knox was their code for Seoras needs to sleep. It had happened less now he was working as a DCI. Sometimes these days, Hope was running, so Macleod got normal hours. But this most recent one had called for a DCI to be taking the reins and took him back to the old days. But you had to sleep. Otherwise, you started drifting off, started contemplating who had the best view at a window.

He shook his head again, made for the stairs and started stumbling down them. He gave a massive yawn as he walked into the old office and saw Ross jump up immediately from behind his desk. Macleod put up a hand.

'Don't,' he said. 'I know where the coffee is. Just keep going.'

Macleod stumbled across. He found his mug and poured himself a coffee. He still had a mug down here, as well as his normal one upstairs. After taking his first sip of a boiling coffee, Macleod turned around to Ross.

'Have you come up with anything?'

'Just checking the rest of the details. I was going to come up and see you, but I wasn't sure if you'd be taking a few minutes.'

Macleod stared over at Ross. 'Just give me the detail.'

'Found a match. I got a name,' said Ross. 'As far as I can tell, it's a Geraint Howles. I had his photograph from a minor misdemeanour. He's quite reckless with a car. He works for a financial insurer in Inverness.'

'Another one on the finance scene. Taybrite was a banker.'

'Howles is a financial insurer,' said Ross. 'He's been with various firms over his time. As far as I can tell, he's a model

53

employee. Taybrite had been a bit of an activist. I'm not seeing that from Howles,' said Ross. 'We could go in and interview some of his colleagues.'

'No,' said Macleod. 'I want to do this quieter. They knew we were onto Taybrite. Maybe they haven't clocked the issue with Howles yet. Maybe he didn't let them know. Taybrite could hardly get away with it. He'd cut his hand. But Howles, it was a photograph from a child, a quick one too. Maybe they don't know about it. I think if they had, they'd have closed the avenue down.'

'Do you want me to talk to Hope, give her the description?'

'Talk to Hope about what?'

Macleod turned to see Hope and Susan Cunningham enter the office. He saw the same bags under Hope's eyes and remembered how he thought of her beauty only in the upstairs office. She certainly looked jaded now. Although in fairness, Cunningham looked worse.

'I'm sending Susan off for a sleep.'

'And you after,' said Macleod. 'Pull in some of the uniform here in case we need the phones manned, but we need some rest. That's an order, Inspector.'

Hope gave a wry smile. 'Anyway, what am I being told?'

'I got a match on the image from the kid's photograph,' said Ross. 'Geraint Howles works for a financial insurer in Inverness. I think the boss wants you to tail him.'

'The boss does not,' said Macleod. 'Hope and Susan had a proper run-in with these people. Their faces will be known. If they get spotted, they could just kill the man. So, I want you to tail him, Ross. Go on, stick on him. Run Cunningham through what she needs to know about what you're doing in case you're out in the field and beyond contactable, then get on to it. I don't want to lose him. He might lead us to a few more of them. Clearly, they will not stop unless we break this open. Given that they've now gone up to multiple killings at a time, our figures will not look very good.

'I take it that's the DCI view,' said Hope. 'Thought we were more concerned about the people.'

'You know what I mean,' said Macleod, but he checked himself. *When did he ever use language like that?*

'I take it I'm meant to get all this information before I go for a sleep,' said Cunningham.

'Who said sleep?' replied Macleod. 'You're covering Ross now.' Cunningham threw a glance at Hope.

'I told you, you'll grow to like him,' she said.

* * *

It had taken Ross two hours to pick up the man's trail in the morning. He wasn't at the financial office, but out with a client. Ross had found out by phoning up and pretending to be someone else. Of course, they didn't know where their client was. Ross made some more phone calls, posing as different authorities to pick up some idea of where the man moved. His habit of a lunchtime swim, which had got delayed until after 2:00, meant that Ross could then tail him back to the insurance office. From there, the man left at approximately four o'clock, arriving at a local Inverness paper.

Ross entered the building as well, asking about placing ads within the paper. He saw that Geraint Howles had been taken through to one of three people working in the office. Sitting within reasonable earshot, Ross found out that Geraint was a contributor to the local crossword, and, in fact, seemed to make up most of the clues. He had popped in with a few deliveries and was lining up the next clues for print next week. Ross grabbed this with bits and pieces as he placed an ad for a completely fictitious tile company.

Just before he left, Ross asked for several copies of the papers over the previous week, just to check through what the ads looked like. He advised the man he was speaking to that he would confirm a booking later. He followed Howles out and tailed him back to his home.

Ross sat one hundred yards up the street with papers splayed over the passenger seat of his car. With each, he pulled out the crossword and filled it in. There was nothing better to do. There was only a break for coffee from a flask and a sandwich he bought just after leaving the station.

Ross sat working through what he thought was one of the easiest crosswords he'd ever done. It wasn't long before he'd completed all seven of the previous week's. Having done so, he now scanned them, setting them beside each other and running through the clues and the answers. It was a shot in the dark, a hunch. He believed that this organisation may be communicating publicly, except you'd need to know what you were looking for.

Geraint Howles was a tall individual, six feet, with blond hair, and looked like an idyllic German. Dressing in a snappy suit, he had shoes that probably had a £200 price tag. He had a car that nipped here and there. In everything, he looked like the well-to-do financial person about town. Yet he was popping in to do crosswords with a two-bit commercial paper. It made little sense. There had to be something in the crossword.

Ross tried to work out what he knew. He knew there'd been an attack and knew it involved hanging. He knew it was against the Allen brothers at the conference with the Holy Glen Hotel. With these things in mind, he scanned the paper.

He didn't know what it was about himself, but Ross had an eye for patterns. He had an eye for things that blended into the background. The easy way to run something like this was to put the first letter of each clue sentence as part of a word. You could have read that and realised what the targets or the location to meet were going to be. The other way, of course, was to put an address in.

Maybe of the person who sent in the clue, for there were crossword clues here attributed to others who had sent them in. According to what was written in the paper, Geraint was merely compiling the crossword, bringing it together. There were credits to certain people.

Ross shook his head. Too obvious, too simple. These people were good, really good. Ross continued to scan. He couldn't explain why, but when he looked at the third word of each clue, the initial letter was jumping out to him. When he took that letter and scrambled it along with the others—correcting the other initial, initials of the third word and the other clues—you could rearrange it and get Holy Glen Hotel. Ross looked at the clues, collected the answers, and took the third letter of all the answers.

Place C, 9:00 PM.

He sat back and let his eyes re-adjust to the world outside, tried to let his brain unravel what he'd just seen. Somebody was putting down code for where to meet, indicating a target. This was clever, and clever on a grand scale, so they could do a waiting game. Ross could pick up the paper every day and try to work out where the next killing would be. Alternatively, maybe there was communication coming in from others. After all, there were credits for people, including addresses. That was a little unusual, surely. You'd maybe give your town, possibly your street, but there was a number there.

Ross called into the station, asking if he could borrow a couple of uniforms to sit and stake out the house. He had investigating to do. He wanted to know what these addresses were. Were they anything? When his cover arrived, it was already beginning to get dark, but Ross was happy. He'd broken into a code. He might find out what was going on, and he would not wait for it. Instead, he would check out these other addresses.

Chapter 08

Ross entered his house with fatigue beginning to tell and was greeted by a child running towards him. He felt little arms grabbing his leg, bent down, picked up their son and gave him a hug before Angus, his partner, stuck his head out from the hallway door.

'Do you want something to eat?'

'No,' said Ross, 'I need my bed.'

'Can you spend a couple of minutes? Daniel's been waiting for you.'

Ross looked down at the eyes looking back up at him. He grabbed the child and walked into the living room, and plonked himself on the sofa. Daniel was pulling at his ears and his nose, then blowing bubbles. Angus asked if he wanted a cup of coffee, to which Ross nodded, and that was the last he remembered.

The morning was sunny, so bright that it woke Ross up. He was still on the sofa in his living room, having slept sitting. This previous night had been a bust. The address given with the crossword had ended up in an empty house on an empty estate. All the same, he'd phoned it in, along with all the other addresses, saying he was going to pick them up in the morning. Macleod had said no. Instead, he'd advised Ross to keep the tail on Howles, picking it up from the people he'd handed it over to the previous night.

The smell of bacon wafted towards Ross's nose. A few minutes later, he was sitting at the breakfast table, forcing himself to eat. Sometimes he just got too dog-tired. He didn't want to do anything, just sleep.

'He's still asleep upstairs,' said Angus, 'But Daniel keeps asking for you. That's a good thing.'

'Is it?' asked Ross.

'But you knew there'd be times like this,' said Angus.

'Yes, I did. We knew.'

'I wasn't complaining. I was being positive.'

'Yes,' said Ross. 'I'll need to shower before I go in. I'll need to . . .'

'Change. How long before you get a proper sleep?'

'I don't know,' said Ross. 'I don't know. Sometimes I wonder if it's a good idea to come home or catch some sleep at the office.'

'It's always good to come home,' said Angus. He put his arms around Ross. 'Be careful.'

'Always,' said Ross. 'Why do you ask?'

'Well, you lost one, didn't you, one of your own? That doesn't happen often. Makes me worried.'

'Yes, it does,' said Ross. He stood up, only half finishing the breakfast and disappeared off to the shower.

Although he felt the water washing over him, he didn't feel like moving. All he could see were letters. This way and that and many combinations. He'd get there. He'd solve it.

At nine o'clock in the morning, Ross took over, dismissing the two constables who'd been watching the house of Geraint Howles. The man hadn't left all evening, but five minutes after

Ross took over, he departed in his car towards his firm. Ross settled down in the coffee shop opposite.

He had a small backpack with him. During the previous night, Susan Cunningham had picked up all the crosswords going back three months. She had dropped off scanned copies to the two constables who'd been watching Howles's house. Ross now had them and sat in the coffee shop working his way through them, waiting to see how Geraint Howles would depart.

The woman in the coffee shop kept bringing the large flask over and pouring Ross more and more coffee throughout the morning. At the fourth time of asking, she stopped beside him, looking down at the crossword.

'You some sort of nut?' she asked.

'Why?'

'You're sitting here in a coffee shop just doing crosswords.'

'It's for competition purposes,' lied Ross. 'At times, I need to get myself up to speed. This is training. I'm out of the way, in a coffee shop. I've got nothing else to do. Nothing else to focus on. I'd do it in a room, but, to be honest, it's not really what I like, to be shut in with the world outside. Here I can see things come and go as I work. Makes the brain go better.'

'The coffee, does that help too?'

'Yes,' said Ross, 'I guess it does.'

'You don't mind me saying it, do you?' said the woman. 'You really could do with getting a life. I'm sure there must be a pretty girl somewhere who'd be interested in you.'

Ross grinned, but he also gave his head a shake, and the woman hurried off. He tried to refocus on the current crossword, but his phone rang.

'Yes, it's Ross.'

'It's Hope. Look, I sent Susan out to check on all those other addresses. All empty. All places have been boarded up. Clearly, there's no one sending these crosswords in except Mr Howles. Looks like it's a dead end from that point of view. You're going to have to stick on him, see what you can get through the crossword, Ross. Or get to people he comes into contact with.'

'Well, he's being thoroughly boring today,' said Ross, 'because he's just sat in that office all day long.'

'Any luck with the crosswords?'

'Working through. Some of the older ones have nothing. Some days have nothing, but we can definitely say that the attack at the Holy Glen was written out in all of them. So Howles then?'

'Seoras wants to see where he takes us. Let us know if you come up with anything else.'

'Will do,' said Ross. He put his head back down, staring at the crossword in front of him.

Ross shifted position for lunch, moving along two doors on the street and having a light salad. He was back, later, at the coffee shop again, crosswords on the table. By one o'clock, Howles hadn't departed.

It must be a quiet day, thought Ross. He sat back in the chair, finding he had to take his eyes off the letters to keep awake. He sat for twenty minutes, simply staring at the street, the people going up and down. Then, in the same way that the words pop out, a figure popped out to him as well.

Five times, the figure had passed in front of the insurance building. There was a man in a black jacket. He had blue jeans on, looked average, possibly like a football supporter. Certainly, there was nothing classy about him, but one thing that Ross did note was he never actually looked at the insurance building. He looked everywhere else as he walked past it. That was unnatural. At some point, he'd see it. At some point, he should stare. Ross quickly packed up the crosswords.

'Had enough for the day, love, have you?'

Ross quickly glanced over and saw the woman coming across with her coffeepot again. 'You don't want any more?'

'No,' said Ross. 'I think I might go out and try to find that pretty girl.'

'Well, you should,' said the woman, shouting at him as he left the cafe.

Ross hit the street and saw the man walking once again by the insurance building. If he was staking out the building, he wouldn't move about this much. You'd find somewhere quiet, somewhere where you wouldn't look like you were constantly on the move. You'd have something else to be doing, like Ross with his crosswords. This man was so obvious, unless he knew Howles was coming out.

Ross popped into a mobile phone shop, which had a large glass window. As he stared out, pretending to check out models, he looked across and saw Howles depart from the building. Sure enough, the man was with him. Ross put down the mobile he was looking at and walked out.

'Did you want to have a better look at it?' said the assistant suddenly.

'No, rubbish,' said Ross, and didn't look back once. Ross followed Howles at a distance, for the man was close behind Howles. He was clearly an amateur, unless Howles knew him, in which case he was running protection. The man was constantly looking around. Ross was clever, though, ducking in and out from behind people. Occasionally, he'd cut down a different street, then double back, coming from another angle.

Ross's jacket was two-sided. Halfway through the pursuit he changed, taking it from a bright blue to a red.

Howles disappeared into a pub, followed by the man. Ross waited for a moment, seeing if Howles would come back out, but when he didn't, he snuck in through another door and could see Howles at the far end of the bar. It was reasonably crowded, but Ross ordered a drink, sat in the corner, and took out a crossword. It was the one he'd been working on.

Howles stayed there for the next two hours, during which Ross worked on the crossword. Slowly, he broke it down and found a message. 'MacQuail's Fishing,' said Ross to himself, 'MacQuail's Fishing.'

He took out his phone and Googled it. MacQuail's Fishing was a conglomerate, with a significant investment portfolio behind it. The fishing was merely the front end of the business, which diversified off into lots of other things that seemed to be much more profitable. Ross continued to work through the crossword and came up with Lollard's Hotel.

When was this going to be? he thought. This crossword was only two days old. The Holy Glen crossword was four weeks old. There was no date for an attack at Lollard's Hotel. Ross went back over the crossword and realised he'd actually got one answer wrong. He looked up with horror. It was going to be tomorrow. He picked up his phone and called Macleod.

'Good work, Ross. I'll get into that. We'll keep it quiet, though. I want you to keep on Howles, see where he goes. Keep swapping over at night, though. Get yourself some rest.'

'Will do, sir. There's just one thing: somebody else is running either protection for him or tailing him as well. It's making it difficult.'

'That's not a problem,' said Macleod. 'You stay with it, at

least you've identified them now.'

Ross put the phone down and continued back to his cross-words. Ten minutes later, he saw Howles leave, but he also watched the other man stand up at the bar and look around. Ross didn't flinch. It was another five minutes before the man left, and Ross disappeared out the side door he'd come in, doubling round the pub and picking up the other man. He followed him slowly, at a careful distance until eventually Howles came back into view.

After a reasonable walk around the city, Howles made it back to the insurance office, where the man walked on past and Ross made his way back over to the cafe. Sitting inside, he watched the man pass up and down six times before he seemed to disappear for the day.

Could they be worried? Ross thought. *They know Howles might have been compromised. If so, is he that important that they want to keep him alive? Why not just dispatch him in the same way that Taybrite had been?*

It was six o'clock when Howles left and went to the sports centre. Ross followed, but he couldn't see the man who had previously run protection for Howles. There was nobody else who seemed to be there to put a shield around Howles. Ross wondered, *had he missed something in the pub? Was there something going down?* It was too late for that. He'd done what he could. Now the important thing was to stay tight with Howles until he could get back to the house for another rest.

His phone rang again, and on picking it up, he found Hope on the other end.

'Anything more to report?' she asked.

'No.'

'Well, we've set up a fast response squad,' said Hope. 'We're going to do it on the quiet. Hopefully, catch them as they come into the conference. Take them in the act, so to speak.'

'I think I may have missed something,' said Ross.

'Why?' asked Hope.

'Somebody ran protection at the office today and then didn't when he went elsewhere. Something went down in the pub, I think, but I'm not sure what.'

'Don't overthink it,' said Hope. 'You've come up with plenty for us. We're in this. We really are, after last time when we couldn't get anywhere.'

'I hope so,' said Ross. 'I really do because I'm getting sick of these long days.'

Chapter 09

Macleod had spent the previous day in quiet meetings sorting out the operation to protect MacQuail's fishing conference. The information in the crossword had been correct and MacQuail's fishing conference was indeed due to start the next day. A large corporate event with different parts of the MacQuail's family and taking place at the Lollard's Hotel on the outskirts of Inverness. Macleod had long discussions, both with the Assistant Chief Constable and those on other teams about whether they should act by cancelling the conference.

Macleod, however, saw this as a great opportunity to step in and nip this in the bud and possibly even get to the bigger organisation behind it. After all the planning and a fitful night's sleep, Macleod was now located inside a van near Lollard's Hotel. The conference was a busy one with over two hundred delegates and Macleod wondered what plan was in place for this mass of people. *What did they intend to do?*

It had been four hours since the conference had opened. The hotel was busy. Watching on CCTV, Macleod could see that the many halls and rooms of the hotel were bustling. Mr MacQuail himself had opened the conference. Macleod had thought that would've been an ideal time for them to pounce, but they hadn't, and instead, everyone had moved off to lunch. They wouldn't gather back into the main room for at least another half an hour.

Macleod had sent Hope out to grab some lunch for himself and her. Cunningham was operating at the perimeter, but his team were sidelined with the potential threat coming. Macleod wanted professional people there. Armed officers knew what to do when the black vans arrived. They should be easy to identify.

There was a phone call and Macleod answered. It was Susan Cunningham.

'Seoras, just had a report from one of the officers watching the far perimeter. Apparently, three white vans seem to be approaching our location.'

'Any more than white vans?'

'No. They pulled past at speed, though. They should be with you any second if they were continuing their previous speed.'

Macleod turned around and advised the head of the armed units, but nothing arrived. Except Hope with a sandwich. They both sat in silence, eating away until one officer watching the perimeter monitor suddenly shouted.

'I got three vans. Black.'

'Where did they come from?' shouted the firearms officer. He quickly started passing instructions to teams. The three vans raced up the driveway of the hotel, then careened up to the side of it. Macleod could see that the conference hall was filling up again. The next session was about to happen.

At the rear of the hotel, three black vans stopped, side doors were opened, and people suddenly jumped out carrying large black plastic cases.

The officer in charge of the firearms team gave the order to go, and Macleod could see them appearing from hidden places, all racing towards the van.

There were calls of 'Police' and 'Stop!' but Macleod saw weapons being drawn. Van doors were closed and shots rang out. Macleod thought someone had been shot in the van, but the vehicles spun round and started heading back out the driveway of the hotel. Some people were now sprinting for cover, but armed officers were also appearing.

Macleod saw the line of spikes across the drive, there to take out the tyres of the van as they looked to escape. A door flew open on the side of the van, shots ringing out from it. Police officers closed, firing back, but one man ran out, seeking to grab the trail of spikes and pull it to one side. The other van spun round, driving at the officers with guns, causing some to run for cover.

Macleod saw a small team of officers racing past those vans, getting close to the main van, from which the man had jumped out to remove the spikes. He was pulling them to one side now, but Macleod saw the officers were getting closer. They were backed up by another small team moving in from the other side, and soon that van was surrounded.

The other black vans had pulled away, the cover now redundant. There were several bodies falling from the van now, and more cries telling people to drop their firearms, but the gunfire continued. As they got closer, the CCTV focused on the van showed someone yelling to someone in the front. It was a cry of desperation, and the man who did it, complete with his mask, stepped out, firing wildly. Macleod saw him being hit twice, falling to the ground just before a massive explosion blew the van apart.

This was no fuel tank blowing up, but a large enough explosion to actually rock the van Macleod was sitting in. Chaos reigned on the monitors. People running here and there, officers down. Macleod could hear shouts across the radio. He knew better than to interfere. This was outside his territory, and he watched in horror as some of his own lay on the ground.

Ignoring the explosion, the other two vans drove off, shots aimed at them. One of them was missing a windscreen. The other looked like its side had been dented in. Whether that was from the explosion or something else, Macleod didn't know.

Inside the hotel was panic. Screams came from everywhere. What had been set up as a nice, quiet job to capture these three vans had gone seriously wrong. They fought back. He hadn't seen that coming.

Vans disappeared out onto the main road with cars following them. There were screams for ambulances. Cries to keep the people locked inside. Macleod could see on the monitor that those in the conference centre were panicking. Many were trying to push to get out, fearing what would come.

Macleod sat back in the seat, his face pale at the images he was looking at. The hotel had turned into a war zone so quickly. He had thought the element of surprise would do it. He had thought he would have something in his hand. Instead, all he had were bodies, and some of them his own.

* * *

'Is he safe out there?'

'I don't know,' said Macleod. 'I think so. He's still on their tail.'

70

Macleod was back at the Inverness Police Station and had received a call from Ross saying that Geraint was on the move. This had happened approximately two hours after the blown capture of the terrorist attack at the conference. Macleod knew Geraint was the only lead they were hanging on to at the moment, but what just happened meant that surely, he would be under suspicion. Ross would have to be good—so good not to get noticed—because if he did, he could be in trouble.

'Where did he say he was going?'

'Out of town into the countryside. We don't know. He's tailing him.'

'Have you been able to contact him, then?' asked Hope.

'No, he might be out of mobile signal.'

'He might be. It might be something else,' said Hope.

'You don't think I'm aware of that, do you? Of course, he could be in trouble.'

The door was rapped. Susan Cunningham didn't wait for an invite. 'Approximately half a mile from the hotel,' she said. 'Lots and lots of white wrapping. Looks like the vans had a white covering, drove in, stripped off quickly before they arrived.'

'Clearly didn't know, though.'

'They'll probably change their method of communication now,' said Hope.

'Yes, they will,' said Macleod.

'We may not even know what.'

'Hope, would you just stop,' said Macleod. 'It's gone wrong. It's gone badly wrong. I'm half inclined to pull Ross out, but I need to know what he's doing and where he is. At the moment, I don't have that. It could also be our best bet to get back into this game.'

71

'What's the ACC say?'

'Jim wants me to go up and see him. I've told him to wait. I need to get this information. The press are all over it out there. Hope, we're up against this one. If Ross can get in, if Ross can find out anything, we might be able to make a move against them.'

'If we don't get in,' said Susan Cunningham, 'we could be in trouble. They didn't stop last time until they picked off all their targets. I can't imagine it.'

Macleod turned away, looked out the window, and then shook his head. *Wasn't the same view, was it?*

'What line do we take now, though?' asked Hope. 'Where else can we go?'

'We go back and see if we can go through their dead.'

'If Jona can put them together,' said Hope. 'There wasn't a lot left after.'

'I saw it,' said Macleod. 'We go back down the trail. See if we can identify them. We find out where they came from. We still haven't got a reason they're doing this. It's to do with the financial sector. Come on, Hope, standard processes, keep going.'

'But it's not standard, is it?' she said. 'It's not. Ross is out in that situation. I'm not happy about this. I'm not.'

Macleod had put his finger up, gave Hope a glare, and then turned to Cunningham. 'Can you give us a minute, Susan?'

'Of course,' she said and stepped outside of the office.

'Don't do that in front of the team. You need to keep it together.'

'Keep it together? That was practically open warfare, Seoras. You saw it. We called it wrong. These people are prepared to die for this. These people are not common thugs.'

'No, they're idealists. I'm getting that,' said Macleod suddenly. 'I'm getting it.'

He picked up a cup and hurled it across the room. It caught his jacket and bounced meekly on the floor.

'Can't even get that right at the moment,' he muttered.

'What are you going to tell Jim?'

'What can I tell him? I've got one officer on a tail. Other than that, we're picking through bodies and rubble to find out who these people are, and each time we do, they seem to get eliminated.'

'I'm going to keep trying Ross. Do you want me to pull him off the tail?'

'No,' said Macleod. 'I don't. We need Howles—need to know where he goes. We have to get into these people, and he's the only thing we've got.'

'Then maybe we should double up on him,' said Hope. 'Put Susan out with Ross or I'll go with him.'

'You can't. You're needed here. Heck, you know that. We can put a constable with him.'

'Given the risk? Are you serious?'

'I'm stretched, Hope. Look at it. Look at what we've got. If it hadn't been for Clarissa, I'd have a team. I could have put one of you onto it. I need somebody streetwise out there, somebody who can handle themselves, somebody that knows when trouble's coming.'

Macleod's desk phone rang. He marched over to it, picking it up. 'Yes? Macleod,' he thundered.

'Jona here. I've got a few names, a few IDs. I've got to make sure it's the actual people who have died. There's just such carnage here. I'll start sending it through. Might be something you can give to upstairs.'

Macleod breathed slowly. 'Good,' he said. 'Anything else you can give me? Anything else I can get as a handle on these people? I'm sick of chasing my tail, Jona. I'm sick of it.'

'Well, there'll certainly be DNA around here,' she said. 'Other than that, I should be able to get some names from the bodies. I'll try to get involved with the weapons, see if we can trace through anywhere they've come from. If we're quick, maybe they won't be able to close the routes. You can take that upstairs as well.'

'Thank you,' said Macleod, putting the phone down.

'Jona?' asked Hope.

'Yes. Possible names, their IDs. Something but not a lot to take.'

The door opened suddenly, and in marched Jim, the Assistant Chief Constable.

'I'm done waiting, Seoras,' he said. 'I'm done. Sit down. We need to talk about this.'

'I'll leave then,' said Hope.

'No. You can sit here with me,' said Jim. 'I need to work out where this investigation is going. At the moment, people are just dying.'

'Well, the first was hardly our fault,' said Hope.

Macleod put his hand up. 'She needs to go, Jim,' he said. 'I've got stuff that needs looked into. I'll talk you through it, but she needs to get on.'

Jim looked over at Hope, then gave a quick nod.

'You can go,' said Macleod.

'You tell me as soon as you hear from Ross, though,' she said.

'Of course,' said Macleod. 'Don't worry, he'll be fine. He's a clever boy. He won't get himself into too much trouble.'

Chapter 10

Ross parked the car, stepped out and followed Geraint Howles as he walked along the Aviemore streets. He seemed to be quite far from Inverness and Ross wondered where he was going, because over these last few days, it hadn't been part of his normal routine. Today, he'd taken a small holdall, thrown it in the back of the car, and driven off from the house. This was in the late evening and Ross was due to hand over shortly, but the activity was so strange, he decided there was no way that he was going to wait.

Of course, the man could always just be going to the sports club, swimming pool, something like that. Something in his routine that Ross didn't know about, but there was no way he was taking the risk. Driving down to Aviemore had seemed strange and Ross had thought several times about phoning Macleod, but really, he had nothing. He was just tailing the man. He could've been going anywhere for any normal reason. There was no need to get excited yet.

Aviemore was fairly busy for the time of evening as Ross watched the man walking along. There was nobody else running cover for him, as far as Ross could see. Ross watched

75

as the man got on the bus some fifty yards ahead of him. As soon as he stepped on board, Ross ran, trying to make sure he covered the distance. He got onboard sitting three rows behind and noted that Geraint Howles still had the holdall with him.

Ross would love to know what was inside. He would love to know where he was going. He hadn't been able to see the front of the bus, but he was still tailing, still able to see his quarry. To have gone back and got the car would've been crazy. He'd have lost the bus in no time, for the car was a good five minutes back.

The bus wound up into the Cairngorms and then stopped down in a valley. Howles had pressed the button to get off the bus in what was an extremely remote area. Ross couldn't very well stand up and get off with him, because where would he be going? Where indeed was Howles going?

Ross surreptitiously glanced out of the window as the bus pulled away, keen to monitor his quarry. As soon as the bus got round the corner, Ross pinged the bell, ran to the front, and started apologising.

'I'm sorry. Sorry, I fell asleep. I need to be off here. I need to be off here.'

'Really?' said the bus driver. 'You seriously want off here? If that's what you want.'

The bus slowed to a halt. 'Thank you,' said Ross.

As he got off, he looked through the windows as the bus pulled away. Was there anyone looking at him? Was there anyone clocking what he was doing? It didn't appear so.

Ross sprinted back down the road, around the corner, but couldn't see Howles. The road went back the way the bus had come, but there were also two paths off it. One seemed to approach a house. Ross was unsure where the other one would go. He could go down to the house, but if that's where Howles had gone, surely he'd still be there by the time Ross got back. Better to first check the other path.

Ross jogged down it, feeling the sweat across his forehead. The path turned this way and that, and Ross had to force himself to slow, as he nearly sprinted round the corner and straight into Howles. He noticed him just in time. Ross stopped and held his breath, although he wanted to breathe in deeply. A small measure of joy rose inside Ross. He still had him. He was still here.

Ross slowed his pace, keeping the man just in sight as they walked down the path. Eventually, it turned towards what he thought was a small copse. Inside, he could see several people, all in the garb of a monk, a grey habit with masks on. Howles had peeled off to one side and Ross could see him getting dressed, removing the monk's habit and mask from his holdall.

Howles didn't approach the copse until he was fully clothed and hidden behind his mask, making Ross wonder if these people knew who the others were? It wasn't uncommon in secret societies. In fact, the fewer people knew about each other, the more difficult it was to break up.

Ross hunkered down behind some bushes and watched as Geraint walked over to the copse. He sat down and a circle was formed. He counted at least ten people there. Then another one arrived along the path behind him, then a third one. He studied the figures carefully.

One was clearly a large woman. Another seemed to have the figure of a female, but this one was more petite. The rest looked like men, but the gowns were so large, it wasn't that easy to be exact. Someone called the session to order, and then the voices became very hushed.

Ross was too far away to hear what was being said. He pulled out his phone and took some pictures. Then he tried to call Macleod. There was no signal. Completely dead. Maybe that was the point. If they were meeting at a place like that, nobody could call for help, nobody could bring in outsiders, nobody could say what was being discussed.

Ross thought for a minute. If he could get close, he might, well, find out what was going on. It would be a risk for if they caught him, he could be dead. This group had already shown that they didn't care and were happy to dispatch innocent people. Previously, it had only been the ministers, but now, well. Ross thought of the four people dispatched at the conference, and they'd certainly killed police officers.

Quietly, Ross strode through the vegetation before him, trying to circle round to where the trees shielded him from sight. Ever so carefully, he crept forward, staying down low, remaining almost in a ball shape. On a bended knee, he crept forward.

As he got closer, he saw the myriad of sticks on the ground, small branches that had been broken off as if being prepped to start a fire. He tried to step around, made a sudden crack as he stood on one, and he heard the voice inside stop talking. Ross strode quickly away, back to the bushes he'd come from.

Just as he settled back into them, he saw a grey figure. He was looking this way and that, checking the perimeter. About three minutes later, he returned inside. Satisfied that no one was about, Ross made his way forward again. This time he chose a slightly different angle to come in at, one that he thought still blocked him from view while avoiding those nasty sticks on the ground. As he got closer, he listened in.

'We screwed up that time,' said a voice.

'Well, someone did. Someone's been followed. They were there waiting for us.'

'Well, it wasn't me.' It was a woman's voice. 'You've been with me. You've checked. I'm not being tailed.'

'Me, neither.' Ross recognised this as Geraint's voice, as there was a slight Welsh undertone. 'You've swept, you've looked, and it's not me. I suggest we get on with our planning.'

'I think you'll find that we don't need to rush. The next one has to go well. Otherwise, it looks like they're getting the upper hand. We lose the fear element. It's more important that we know how they knew. We need to know where it's come from. We need to know if there's a traitor in our midst.'

'When's the next one?'

'It'll be posted out as per usual. We'll then be selecting and we'll put plans into motion. We need some of the rest of you to step up. Cover those we have lost.'

'About that,' said another man's voice. 'They're going to know who those people are now. They can put it back together . . . DNA.'

'The ties have already been cut,' said the man who had opened the meeting. His voice was strong and calm, but not reassuring. 'We don't know who each other is. We only know a few, and that's how it stays. Those with ties to the dead men have been cut off.'

'Has the target been picked?' This was a female voice. 'Because I want to be involved in the next one. I've stood back too long.'

'You are where you need to be. I plan it. I called this meeting not to have a discussion about our next target. There are plenty of financial institutions ready. It's all been corrupt. We will go through them one by one. Our list is eight long. We've made a success with one. We've failed with another, but we'll come back to it. Trust me, we will. Our ranks are swollen and we have plenty of time. What we have is a detective on our back.'

'Who?' asked the voice.

'Same one. Macleod. Always Macleod.'

'There are reasons to bring Macleod in himself,' said a voice.

Ross was astonished at the suggestion. Reasons to bring Macleod in. What could they be?

'He was there. His name was mentioned, and we will come to that. He's still on the case. He's still coming after us. Even getting his win last time didn't do it. He still wants more. He knew we wouldn't stop, but we need to clean house first. Then it will be posted. We've come out here to the middle of nowhere, much harder to be tailed, and none of you have been. Well, except for one of you.'

Ross's skin went cold. Inside, he felt numb. Who were they talking about?

'Which one of us?' asked a voice. 'Can you tell us which one of us has been followed?'

'I don't know,' said the man, 'because he doesn't know who was on the bus. He doesn't know where people are being dropped off, but someone got on a bus last minute and then raced off, desperate to be clear. I suspect he'll be listening now. He should take in all we've said. That's why I mentioned the next job. That's why I brought him in.'

'I looked outside, there was no one.'

'This time we will all look!' Ross heard a commotion. People standing up. He didn't wait. He turned and ran. As he reached the path back towards the road, he heard a shot and something whistled just above his head.

'Bloody hell,' said Ross under his breath, and he ran for all he was worth. Legs pounding, knees lifting high. He swerved along the path this way and that. There were sounds behind him, but as he turned the path towards the road, he saw a car pull up in front.

It could've been somebody else. It could've been a coincidence, but Ross was not taking any chances. He turned right off the path and crashed through the undergrowth. He heard dogs get out of the car, and Ross legged it for everything he had. As he continued to run, birds lifted from the surrounding undergrowth, clearly giving his position away.

He cut back, heading more towards the road again, but then he caught sight of a grey figure somewhere up ahead. He turned right again, crashing through the undergrowth towards anywhere that there wasn't anyone, just wanting to be away from them. It was then that he saw the grey figure ahead of him. He looked left and saw another one. Ross crouched down quickly.

'Come out. Come out, little rabbit, wherever you are. We're going to string you up. We're going to find out who you work for and string you up. You will not survive this one.'

Ross slowly crept forward. There was a grey figure up ahead, but it had its back to him, and Ross slowly crept along. He was only six feet away from the figure, passing by behind it. He stayed down low as he saw the figure turn, looking to scan through the undergrowth. Ross was down on his belly and praying that he wasn't seen. Slowly, he crept forward, arms and knees driving through the vegetation.

'Come on, now,' he said to himself, but he could feel his knees shaking. Every part of him was in terror. He had his troubles during his time working for the police, none more than when he'd been shot working in the Monarch Isles. But these people, they wouldn't simply shoot you. There was good reason to believe that they would do more than kill him. Instead, they would torture him first. He'd seen the people hanged at the hotel.

As Ross crept forward, the arms in front of his head suddenly hit something solid. He could hear water. Slowly, he lifted himself up. It was an old stone wall. As he crept up and peered over the top, he realised it was a broken viaduct. Down below was a river. It may have been deep, but he wasn't sure. It was certainly flowing fast, and it may whisk him down the valley.

Ross could feel the hands shaking as he peered down, trying to estimate if he'd survive the jump. The fall was a good thirty feet, if not more. Would the water be enough down there? There were rocks on either side. A channel down the stream? He wasn't sure. There was thrashing now in the undergrowth behind him.

'Come out, little rabbit. Where are you? We know you're here. We know you're about.'

Ross bent down again, trying to weigh up his options, but his mind was racing. At the back of it were Angus and Daniel. It couldn't end like this, could it? They'd fought so hard to be a family, and now he was cornered. He'd let himself get stuck in a position where he was alone.

Ross heard them moving. Knives swatting away the vegetation, cutting it back. It was damp from rain earlier on in the day and his clothes were soaking. He needed to do something. He couldn't get back out to the road. They had cut that off.

'The dogs have a scent,' said someone suddenly. 'The dogs have a scent. Go! Hunt!'

Ross heard the undergrowth crash, the dogs racing forward. He couldn't see them yet, but he knew they must be getting close. What sort were they? What would they do? If they got a hold of him, he couldn't get away.

Ross desperately looked around. Grey figure that way, grey figure this way. I can't outrun a dog, anyway. There was a woof followed by another one. Suddenly, a dog broke through the vegetation and made a snap for Ross's leg. He was fortunate it hadn't grabbed the leg, but Ross was now in its grasp. Another dog was arriving.

There was no time to think. No time to wonder what to do. Ross kicked out with his spare leg, catching the dog that had hold of him right between the eyes. It whimpered, letting go briefly, and Ross grabbed a hold of the wall with his hands and threw himself over.

He twisted and started descending the thirty feet down on his back. The water caught him by surprise, suddenly enveloping him, but also delivering a large pain across his spine. There was no time to wonder, no time to think about what had happened, as the current dragged him. It took him down at first, before throwing him up off the side of what could've been a small waterfall.

His head went under again, and he fought hard. When he did surface, he heard barking, but Ross pushed himself back into the flow of the river. He sped along, racing downward, on and on, until eventually he sailed out off a drop, falling down what must have been another twenty feet. He crashed into the water below.

As he pulled himself up to the surface, gasping for air, he could feel his body shaking. He'd been that close. That close to them having him. He swam over as best he could, pulled himself out on the rocks. There, twenty metres, he could see the road.

Maybe it followed the river. Maybe they would come down. Would the dogs be able to pick up a scent?

Ross continued into the undergrowth, and got close to the road. He crouched down as a car came towards him, but rather than flag it down, he let it go. They could be in cars. They could be anywhere. Then he saw a campervan approach.

It had a foreign plate. *Belgium,* he thought. Ross stepped out of the undergrowth, waving his arms, and a terrified man in the driver's seat slammed on his brakes. Ross reached inside his jacket, pulled out a heavily soaked warrant card, and pushed it up to the window.

'Police,' he said, 'Police.'

A woman opened the door, and he stepped inside. 'Aviemore,' he said, 'Aviemore.'

'Yes, Aviemore,' said the bemused man. Ross sat back breathing heavily with his new European allies, trundling along the roads at just over thirty miles an hour heading for Aviemore.

Chapter 11

'Did you speak with him?' Macleod asked Hope.

They were standing in Macleod's office and the man looked nervous. It wasn't a common thing for him, but Hope could tell something was bugging him. With Seoras, that usually meant that something was about to happen that he didn't want. This case had been a long haul already. Hope didn't believe they had got very far. It wasn't just the recent events. It was all the incidents over four months ago. Clarissa leaving, Patterson still working through his recovery. Macleod was carrying it all up on his shoulders because they didn't get them—didn't get those who'd done it. Now the killers were back.

There was no use in recriminations. Seoras had told her that. He couldn't go back over what was done. All he could do was go on, but he was going back. Sometimes you knew all the good advice to give someone else, and you could probably give it to yourself, but people didn't listen to themselves. People didn't listen to their body when it said, 'Slow down. This is too much. Are you truly sleeping?' or, 'This job's going to kill you.'

People didn't listen, and she got the feeling that Macleod

wasn't listening now.

'I didn't hear from him. I went to see him. He's good. He'll be okay, but it was a close call. It's not like Ross to be shaken up. Reminded me a bit of the time when he was shot.'

Hope watched Macleod turn back to the window, gazing out of it vacantly. It was a habit she'd seen many times before. A habit that, in truth, was a good thing, for it gave him time to reflect. Right now, he looked more vacant than ever before, out of ideas. That wasn't Seoras. Seoras was a leader. Seoras knew where to go. Even when they were scrambling around in the dark, he pushed forward the ideas of what to do.

'Did he find out much?'

'Not a lot, but you can ask him yourself,' said Hope. 'He'll be in shortly. I told him to have a late morning. Ross was a while getting checked over last night. He fell some distance into a river and then got washed down and away. He picked up some photographs as well, but they weren't much use. They didn't tell us anything else.'

'Have we got a tail on Geraint Howles again?'

'Sent uniform round to the ones who were keeping watch through the night in place of Ross. The man hasn't come out of his house.'

'We may have to pick him up,' said Macleod. 'He'll know that people are onto him, but we'll watch him first. Watch him find out.'

'Well, he hasn't left the house since. Whenever Ross got back, I realised he would not take over. I sent uniform round, and the car was already there.'

'Well, what exactly happened last night?'

There was a knock at the door.

'This might be it,' said Hope and strode across to Macleod's door. She opened it, revealing Ross standing on the other side. He was, once again, dressed in a smart suit. Looking at him, you hardly would've known of his adventures the day before. The bruises were probably on the back and other places because his face looked fine. Yet when Hope looked into his eyes, she could see a hollowness inside.

'Come in,' said Macleod. 'Sit down, Ross. Do you need coffee?'

'I can get you, sir.'

'I have a secretary up here,' he said to Ross. 'You don't have to pander after me.' Hope saw the slightly hurt look on Ross's face as Macleod marched past and ordered several coffees. On his return, he stood and stared at Ross for a while.

'Are you okay?'

'I'll live,' said Ross. 'There's some bruising on my back. It's sore today. The odd cuts and bruises. Got a new pair of trousers as well. Dog ripped them to shreds.'

'Well, run me through it,' said Macleod, taking a seat.

Ross took Macleod through tailing Howles to Aviemore, and the bus that followed. He realised that he'd been seen possibly by the bus driver or someone on it. He then spoke about being chased, his voice going quiet when he mentioned the dog taking hold of his trousers, quieter still, when talking about the drop. Then Ross picked up again, mentioning the foreign couple. They drove him back into Aviemore.

'Sensible,' said Macleod, 'waiting like that, making sure it wasn't one of them.'

'They were ready to kill me,' said Ross. 'I'm convinced of that. They would've tortured me at first. Things seem to have stepped up. Things seem to be . . .'

'Personal,' said Macleod.

'Personal,' said Hope. 'How personal?'

'Personal in they're coming after us. They never did that with the ministers. It wasn't about us. Patterson wasn't an attack on us. Patterson was in the way. They were scrapping, fighting for their lives. The idea that you've been infiltrated by a police officer and you wouldn't just flee. Instead, you're coming after him. They also sent a message to us last time. They warned us. Becoming personal, Hope. Criminals are usually dispassionate. The ones who are working for the money, the prestige, for some financial gain. The lunatics make it personal,' said Macleod.

'There's still the watch on my house,' said Ross. 'Thank you for that, sir.'

'Don't thank me. This job put you into that situation. I just hope that Angus and the wee one are safe, being looked after.'

'I told Angus they were there,' said Ross, 'but he hasn't been able to see them. They're very good at staying discreet.'

'Very good,' said Macleod. 'Jane hadn't picked up on them either. I did.'

Hope noticed that he turned away, looking to the window. Never had she seen Seoras's hand actually tremble. It was a very dull shake, not an instant panic. More of a building tide, something that was sweeping in and beginning to occupy his mind, something that was shaking him to the core.

'Where do we head from here then?' asked Hope.

'Well, what are your thoughts?' asked Macleod. 'You're the DI now. Where do we go, Hope?'

'I'm for bringing Geraint Howles in. Sweat him in here. Maybe they'll realise that he's the one that was tailed. Then they'll think about it. You know what they're like. They saw what happened to Andrew Taybrite. They weren't long getting

88

rid of him. It's ironic, isn't it? They opened up their group, and now they're having more problems trying to control it.'

'Always the way,' said Macleod. Then he turned to Ross, 'Are you okay—to continue, I mean? You were pretty roughed up last night.'

'If I'm here, I'm okay. You don't have to ask, sir.'

'I've already asked him,' said Hope. 'I don't think any of us are on top form at the moment, but we've got a job to do.'

'I think you're right,' said Macleod. 'We've played the Howles's card. We've tailed them. We've found a group of them meeting, twelve of them.'

'It's too big a number to round up, twelve, isn't it?' asked Ross.

'More like fifty,' said Macleod. 'He's operating in a sizeable group. He'll be operating it with measures in place. Andrew Taybrite was killed off. Few people would've known about him; otherwise, the entire group would've had to be held together. No, I reckon he's running it like they did in World War II, the spy networks, only so many people knowing each other. Bring them in together. You heard them talking, Ross; there were the newspapers; they were going to be putting out the jobs again; what was going to happen. He doesn't need to do that if it's only one person who's then contacting the entire team. You need to do that when everybody's displaced from each other, and everybody doesn't have good lines of communication. I'm wondering do they even know each other. Maybe there's just the one central figure, and that's who we need to get.'

'You said it was personal,' said Hope. 'You think it's personal for him or her?'

'No, not specifically,' said Macleod. 'Something's not right with that because we had people before talking about abuse as they're growing up. We're now looking at possible financial sector abuse or irregularity, something's that's hurt people. We need to find out what that common factor is. But why go from one to the other?' asked Macleod. 'Why do that? And what is this constant harping about my time at Stornoway.'

'You said that was a decoy, and you're telling me it isn't?'

Hope stared at Macleod. Several years ago, she never would've asked a question like that, but from what he'd just said, the point had to be put out there. Was he telling the truth? After all, he was the one who had gone off to investigate his past. He was the one who had gone to see McNeil, to the retirement home. He had covered off all that side of the investigation, and here was Hope questioning the man who had built her career over the last year or two.

'Nothing happened out there,' said Macleod. 'Nothing that I was involved in, but I'm glad you asked the question. We need to ask every question. There's something personal in this,' said Macleod. 'I thought it was a distraction. I thought he was . . . I thought it was a case of . . . that's why I had stopped.'

'What?' asked Hope. 'What?'

There was a loud rap at the door. Before Macleod could say anything, it was flung open to reveal his secretary. 'Seoras,' she said. 'Seoras, Janes's been shot.'

'What?'

'Shot,' said Linda. 'Angus, too,' she said, turning to Ross.

'Hope, get . . .' For a moment, Hope thought Macleod was going to crumble. His police instinct had taken over. 'Get units there. Contain the situation, deal with it.'

Then she saw the other side, the side that suddenly realised his partner had been shot. His partner might be in real danger, critical.

'What's the situation with them?' asked Hope quickly, standing to take charge.

'On the way to the hospital. I don't know their condition,' said Linda.

'Seoras, Ross, go. Go to the hospital.'

Macleod stood up, ran to grab his coat, and took off with Ross. As they descended the stairs, Hope ran behind them. She spotted a constable she knew.

'McLaughlin, take the DCI and the DC to the hospital now.'

Raigmore Hospital was only over the road from the police station. Not far at all, but Hope wanted somebody with them, in case they broke down, in case things got to them so much. Someone who could talk back to her, somebody who could relay things, deal with the situation.

She watched the two men running down the stairs, but she strode quickly behind them. She followed them into the car park, watched as the constable got in, started the car, and reversed it to drive away. Macleod looked at her through the car window. He was pale, so very pale. She didn't clock Ross's face as the car pulled away.

Think, Hope, she said to herself. *Think.* The blood was pumping through her veins. Seoras was compromised. Ross wasn't there to lean on. *Bloody Clarissa*, she thought. *Why did you leave us? Why did you leave us when we need you?*

No, she decided. *No, come on.* Hope tore back up to her own office to find Cunningham and several constables working behind their desks.

'Susan, Seoras's partner's just been shot, so was Angus, Ross's partner. We need to bring Geraint Howles in. Get hold of the officers there who are on stakeout. Tell them to bring him in now.'

Hope's mind was racing. If they'd done this, had they realised Ross was the tail from Macleod? Did they realise they had been tailed, how he'd got there? Had he been under observation? If they had . . . Hope left the main office and tore into her own. She picked up the phone and called the Assistant Chief Constable.

'Yes, it's Jim.'

'Jim, it's Hope. Jane's been shot; Angus, too. That's Ross's partner. Don't know how bad yet. I've got a potential suspect that may be compromised as well. I can't deal with Macleod at the moment. Can you get over, sort that side of it out for me?'

'Of course. I'll take it they've gone to Raigmore?'

'Yes,' said Hope. 'Thanks, Jim.'

'Keep me informed,' he said, and Hope put the phone down. As she did so, there was a knock at her office door. Susan Cunningham walked in slowly.

'What?' asked Hope. 'What's the matter?'

'Geraint Howles is dead.'

'How?' asked Hope.

'Officers knocked on the door, then saw somebody swinging in one of the rooms. Broke in. It looks like suicide.'

'Dammit,' said Hope, slamming her fist into her desk. 'Dammit.' Then she stopped. 'Your close family, Cunningham.'

'What?'

'We need a security detail on them. Once you've done that,' said Hope, standing up, 'we've got two crime scenes to get to and we've got to work out what's next, because they've just closed us off again. They've just damn well closed us off.'

'Give me a minute,' said Susan. Hope turned around and looked out the window, waiting for her DC to come back.

Outside the window, as she looked across Inverness, she saw women pushing buggies, men walking here and there, kids playing in parks. After about a minute, she turned away.

'What on earth did Seoras ever see in that view?' she spat out loud.

Hope felt her body suddenly stop shaking. After an incredible outpouring of fear and panic had gone through it, she felt drained and thought about the enormity of where she now stood. This was going to be on her. This case was going to be on her, a case that Macleod had got nowhere with.

Chapter 12

Macleod felt like somebody had taken his guts and spilled them on the street in front of him. He felt empty in his core, a hollowness that he was struggling to even begin to comprehend. The doctor had said so little. She was in the theatre and they were working on Jane. The bullet was close, too close, and they had to operate immediately to protect her organs. She'd lost a lot of blood. There was a genuine danger he could lose her.

Ross had been more fortunate. Angus had been hit in the shoulder. The protection guarding the house had been knocked unconscious prior to the attacker coming to the door and shooting Angus in the shoulder. But they hadn't done a very good job of incapacitating those watching. Instead, the protection unit had recovered and intervened by throwing something just as the person was about to shoot. They'd hit them towards the back of the head. The gun had missed its target, but Angus's shoulder was a mess.

Ross had disappeared back to the house where their child was still there. Having known that Angus was going to be okay, Ross did his first duty as a father.

Macleod felt alone. People were rushing back and forward.

People kept going here and there. Sure, people smiled at you, but they didn't know what was going on in your life, and those doctors and nurses who did, didn't smile in the same way. It was that almost grimace of 'We can't say anything, but it's not looking good.'

It had been three, maybe four hours since his arrival, and Macleod had walked up and down this corridor several times. He'd gone to phone Hope occasionally, but he couldn't even hold the phone. The constable with him told him to sit, told him to not worry about investigations, told him Hope would deal with it. He didn't need to be told that; he knew that, but what else was he to do? They were operating on Jane. He couldn't do any of that. But he could help with the investigation. He could get involved in that. Who was he kidding? He was a wreck. He was truly a wreck.

Macleod heard the door at the far end of the corridor open and then the clip of boots, confident strides, and he looked up to see a figure with a swishing ponytail. The tall woman continued at pace along the corridor before slowing as she approached him. He tried to give Hope a grin but failed.

'Seoras,' said Hope. He just stood there, and she ran up to him, threw her arms around him, and held him tight. 'What's the news?' she asked.

'She's . . . She's . . .' He couldn't speak.

'Jane's in theatre. She's got a bullet near to vital organs. They're operating to deal with it.'

'She's lost a lot of blood as well,' said the constable, who'd come with Macleod.

Hope nodded. 'She'll be good,' she said, but not confidently. Macleod could hear the tremor in her voice.

'Where's Ross?' asked Hope.

'Angus is going to be okay,' said Macleod.

'Well, that's good. That's good, Seoras, isn't it?'

Macleod tried to nod, but his thoughts weren't there. They were with Jane. He almost felt bad because part of him couldn't have cared less about Angus. It's all about Jane now. Jane was the important one.

'DC Ross went home,' said the constable to Hope. 'Had to look after his child. He was happy Angus was going to be okay.'

'Well, that's sensible,' said Hope.

Macleod heard another set of footsteps clipping up the hall. He looked down and saw another woman, not as tall, but with a ponytail, but this time, blonde hair. She really was cut in Hope's image, he thought.

Hope turned to Susan Cunningham and quickly explained the situation to her.

'Let's hope she's going to be okay then, Seoras,' said Susan. The woman stood, not knowing what to do. Macleod realised some response was required, though he was cold inside. 'Thank you,' were the only words he could manage.

He turned, reached for Hope, buried his head into the front of her shoulder. Because of her height, he couldn't get up and place his head fully on, but he flung his arms around her. She held him tight, so very tight.

In that moment, she was like a life ring. He felt like he was stuck out in the middle of an ocean, drifting away, unsure what direction the current would take him, but clinging onto this ring around him. As long as he could cling onto that ring, he'd end up somewhere. He'd be all right. His life ring, a six-feet, redheaded woman. His mind flashed back to when he first met her, first worked a case with her.

'I'm sorry,' he said, and tears flowed.

'It's okay,' said Hope, but he knew she did not know what he was talking about. He'd seen her as a Jezebel, somebody loose, somebody who wasn't of his standing, yet at the same time, part of him had hungered for her. Now here she was, his rock, his lifeline, who he had treated so badly, and yet here she was.

'I'm sorry,' he said again, crying into her shoulder.

People always said that he wasn't an emotional man—that he was stone cold. He could chew out any of the up-and-coming constables; he could take on those up-above chief constables, DCIs in his day, anyone that wasn't pulling their weight, anyone who wasn't getting to the truth. Macleod was nails. Macleod was hard, cold, and that's how he got to where he got. That's how he cut through all the nonsense and found out about what people really were.

Nobody understood he was a deeply emotional man. All his feelings were there under the surface, and sometimes they raged. Now, they were just a mess, sending him this way and that, thoughts reeling in his mind, just desperate for his Jane to come back to him.

It took a while before Macleod realised he was still being held. Cunningham was standing awkwardly, a little embarrassed at the scene in front of her.

'Let's take a seat, Seoras,' said Hope. She turned to the constable, who had come with him. 'Can you get me a sandwich or something from the cafe? Cunningham, you want anything?' There was a nod of her head, and Hope reiterated, 'Two sandwiches. Actually, get a third one for Seoras. One for yourself. Coffee, drink. Just . . . Just get stuff from the cafe. Yeah?'

She watched the woman turn to go. 'Thank you,' she said. Macleod looked up at Hope and saw her tear-stained face.

'We'll get through this,' she said. 'She'll be all right.'

'You don't know that,' he said suddenly and bitterly. 'No one knows that. They came for my Jane.'

'You're right,' said Hope quietly, 'but we'll get through this, you and me.'

Macleod nodded and sat in silence with Hope until the constable had returned with a sandwich and some drinks. He was handed a cup of tea. *I must be unlucky today*, he thought, but not because of what happened to Jane. His mind suddenly wondered how this woman didn't know he liked coffee. Everyone at the station knew it was coffee. He sipped it anyway. He hated tea, but it jarred him, jarred him back away from himself, back towards the stone-cold detective.

'Where are we?' he asked Hope. 'Where's the investigation now? I'll need to brief Jim.'

Jim had been there before Hope arrived. He was a good Assistant Chief Constable. Jim was caring; he was thoughtful, but he wasn't what Macleod had needed, and after that was clear, Jim had left.

'We're struggling,' said Hope. 'Geraint Howles hanged himself. Every time we get close, they close the loop. Sometimes they close it themselves. It's like . . .'

'Like they're in some sort of pact, like they're tight in, like the whole is much more important than themselves,' said Macleod.

'And they must be passionate about it,' said Susan.

'They must be passionate about it to come after me,' said Macleod. He had soaked up the comfort from Hope, and now the old dog was kicking back. He was rising.

'Ross said that they'd be contacting again. Alternative papers,' said Hope. 'They've got to be doing the same type of system. You don't just suddenly throw a new one in, but they'll be doing it in different papers. There'll be a connection, there'll be a way to contact. We have to get into that. We need to find it.'

'Connection,' said Macleod. 'Ross needs to come and start looking again. We need him working on the crosswords. I need him working on connections.'

'We're going to get names of people. Get descriptions of who attacked Jane and Angus.'

'You mean when they were in robes?'

'No,' said Hope, 'but they came with the masks on.'

'Equipment. We need to find their supplier of equipment. We need to find that. Get more people. Expand the team. If there's a problem, tell me. I'll get hold of Jim.'

'I've spoken to Jim. And I'll do it again,' said Hope. 'You need to be here. You're compromised. This is on me,' said Hope.

'It's on us.' Susan Cunningham had chipped in from behind them. 'We'll get them, Seoras. We'll get them.'

'I'll call Ross,' said Macleod.

'I can do it,' said Hope.

'No,' said Macleod. 'I'll do it. We've both just suffered. If it comes from you, it's wrong. Strictly, he needs to rest, and you need to give that message. Me? I'm in a different place. He'll take it from me. He won't deny me.'

'That's why it should come from me,' said Hope.

'Gloves are off, Hope. I mean it. Gloves are off, but I can't think straight. I need you for that. I need you to do what you do, the dogged stuff. Pick up the threads. Break them down. Get after them. You don't think how I do, but you need to think how you do. You need to get in and unravel the threads.'

He turned and looked at the far wall. He was fighting back the tears. There were now footsteps coming up the corridor again. Most of the hospital staff wore soft shoes, sensible things for running around on your feet all day. The women on his team all seemed to enjoy boots, but these boots made a slightly different clop. The walk was easier, less of a determined stride, more of a practised ease about the way the sound came across. Macleod didn't have to look to know who it was, but when he turned, he saw the familiar tartan shawl, the trews underneath. There was a face like thunder coming towards him. He stood up and approached Clarissa.

'How is she?'

Macleod couldn't speak. Talking about Jane, talking about the situation, the possibilities or not, flummoxed him.

'It's not good,' said Hope behind Macleod. 'It's life and death, Clarissa. Good to see you, though.'

'Was it them?' she asked.

'Yes,' said Hope. 'The ones with the masks. They shot Jane at close range. They also shot Angus.' Clarissa's face at first fell and then tightened. Macleod could see the pain and anger pouring into that expression.

'They shot Ross's man with the kid, with his kid there?'

'Yes,' said Hope.

Clarissa turned away and for a moment seemed to wander around. When Macleod looked at her, she wasn't looking back. Her eyes were far off in the distance, but there was nothing to see in the hospital corridor. Then, suddenly, she walked forward to Macleod, wrapped him up in an enormous hug, and whispered in his ear, 'I'll get the bastards.'

She stepped by, turned to Hope, and gave a nod.

'Take care of him,' said Clarissa, and she turned and marched back down the corridor. This time there was no lilt in the step. Macleod could see her shoulders were raised. He hoped to

God she didn't do something stupid.

Chapter 13

Hope would've stayed all day with Macleod, for the surgery was going to drag on. Jane was stable, but critical. It was one of those phrases that was hard to be confident about. Yes, it could have been worse. She could have been dead, she could have been failing, or she could have been unstable and critical. Medical terminology just didn't cut it for those who were waiting.

Hope had a job to do and, together with Susan, she'd returned to the station to the main office. There was only Susan Cunningham from the primary team. The assistant chief constable had pushed as many people as possible towards her. Yes, Hope knew them from about the station, but she didn't know them that well. This wasn't her team. This was people pitching in as best they could.

Hope organised a search of all papers across Scotland, local or national, asking that all crosswords be pulled together. She'd received a phone call from Ross. He was going to have to stay at home, needing to look after his wee one. But he was offering his services. Hope wasn't one hundred percent happy with what Macleod had done. She didn't agree that Ross should have been put under pressure and she realised Macleod hadn't asked her to call him to do it, because she wouldn't have.

Part of her was scared seeing Macleod the way he was. This determined, angry man. Usually, Macleod was detached. He could be methodical about it. Yes, he got annoyed, but this seemed to have riled up something in him. She didn't blame him. This was Jane. Macleod and Jane were as close as anyone she knew. Macleod had no kids, no extended family. Jane was everything—the one thing above the team that Macleod prized, a woman who was vivacious, vibrant, and brought out the best in the man.

Hope had also taken a call from Jim to say that he put plenty of protection around her own partner. John would turn around and say, 'No, we don't need it. It wasn't essential.' John didn't know about stuff like this. Hope kept a lot from him. He'd been attacked once in the hospital. This was way beyond that.

'Excuse me, Hope.'

She realised she'd been staring across the open office and one of the uniformed constables was approaching her.

'Yes, Jackie.'

'Been doing a trawl through recent reports just to see if there's anything, and there was a call from a local newspaper in Oban, into the station. They logged that a man was unhappy and threatening. The editor had a rather strange situation to do with a submitted crossword and a man raging at him. Just thought it sounded . . . well.'

'Sounds like it's worth a conversation,' said Hope. 'Give me the number of the paper.'

Hope retired to her office, sat down, and went to make the phone call. There was no coffee. Normally, there would be coffee waiting.

Ross was missing. Ross wasn't there. What was it Macleod always said about Ross? He picked up all the loose ends. Picked up anything that wasn't happening. He made sure that everything operated. Hope stood up, walked to the door of her office, and called for Jackie to come in.

'Jackie, I've got a very important job for you.' The woman looked at her, a bit bemused. 'Coffee. Make sure everyone has coffee. Also, make sure that there's plenty of food out there for everyone to eat. If you see something that's not happening, you do it.'

'Excuse me?' said Jackie. 'You just told me to make everyone coffee.'

'Yes,' said Hope.

'That's not my job,' she said. 'I don't drink coffee. I don't do coffee.'

'Jackie, you're not usually on this team like most of the people out there, but we are a team and one of the key people on this team is DC Ross. He's brilliant on the computers, but more than that, he's our sweeper.'

Jackie looked at her immediately again and Hope could see the cogs going round and round. 'You mean he cleans up?' said Jackie. 'There's staff at the end of the day.'

'No,' said Hope. 'Listen, he's our sweeper. If anything isn't happening on the team, he's doing it. He makes sure that everybody's okay. He's the first one to bring attention if somebody's struggling. We're working a tough case, one that's caused injury to our police family. I don't get to be the eyes and ears in here as I've got an investigation to run. I want you to get amongst your colleagues, make the coffee, make sure everyone out there is okay. If they're not, I want to know. It's what Ross does for me. It's what Ross did for Macleod. This is not a slap. You've been given one of the most important jobs here.'

She thought Jackie almost smiled for a moment and then she looked at Hope. 'I don't do coffee.'

'Learn,' said Hope. 'Seriously, learn. You can start with mine.'

Hope picked up the phone and called the number for the local newspaper in Oban.

'Hello. Yes, I rang up before. The local station. Who's this?'

'My name's DI Hope McGrath. I'm calling from Inverness. I need to speak to you about the information you reported, sir.'

'Inverness. It's a bit serious for what I'm saying.'

'I don't need to tell you, sir, why it's me that's calling. I just need information from you. Can you relay the story to me again?'

'I will do,' said the man. 'My name is Daniel Burrows. I put the newspaper out here, but I don't contribute everything that's in it. I do most of the local stories. Occasionally, I'll pick one or two up from some of the other journalists, but we have a crossword section in the back and for that, people write in.

'Now, to be honest, there's not that many. Recently, in the last six months, a man called Murray started contributing to them. They're good crosswords. They're very good. Right at our level. Not too difficult to get the answers. We don't do crosswords to find the next member of Mensa. We're doing crosswords for fun.'

'I understand that. You said it was just over six months ago?'

'Yes. He would send them in pretty regularly. Sometimes, with something like that, you'd expect people to come with a whole pile of them. They would give them to you and then say, look, just put them out over the next while, whatever. Because you don't get any money for this. This is for fun.'

105

'But Murray didn't do that?'

'No. They came in tiny dribs and drabs, maybe the odd one or two. He also would get at me to put them out within the next day or two. Said he just liked to see them that way. He said it was an autistic thing. I've got to be honest, I found nothing autistic about the man at all. Well, I don't have a glut of crosswords. Somebody like this supplying them that well, you just do what they ask because then they keep feeding you.'

'You had a problem with him.'

'Yes,' said Daniel. 'I had a problem with him. He phoned up after he'd sent some crosswords in saying he wanted this one in for the next day. I said to him, no, because I'd already lined up that one for that day. I wasn't being awkward; it was just I'd done it, set the paper up. The paper was ready to go to pre-print, and that was that.'

'He didn't take kindly to your rebuke?'

'No. Murray came in. He actually came into the building and at first, he kept pushing. Could I do it? Then he offered me money. Well, I'm not taking money. It's wrong. This is a voluntary thing, the crossword. If I get money involved, well, then I have to talk about these contributors to the paper? I have to pay them differently. They have to report that pay. I just, oh, it's just too much hassle. I said that to him and I said, 'I'll put it in the day after.''

'What did he say to that?'

'Well, he grabbed me by the throat, pulled me up over the table. I'm not a big man and neither is he, but blimey. I thought he was going to smash my face in.'

'You get his name, his first name, I mean.'

'David Murray, the man passed on an address. If you can, let me know how you get on.'

'Well, I'm not sure I can do that at the moment, but thank you for your help.'

'Well, if there's anything else you need,' said Daniel, 'just come back to me.'

'Are you still printing his crosswords?'

'He's still sending them in. We haven't really spoken since, but they still come in by post. Like I say, I don't have a glut of them, so I use them. But if he comes back in the office, he's getting told to get the hell out. Don't take kindly to being threatened.'

'I'm sure you don't. If he comes back in the office, however, phone immediately to here, please.' Hope passed a mobile number on to Daniel. 'It's very important.'

'What's he done?' asked Daniel.

'You're a reporter, so I'll tell you this. I can't talk about that at the moment. We're in the middle of an investigation.'

'DCI Hope McGrath, you're that one that works with Macleod, aren't you? You'll be on this big case. The murders that are happening.'

'If you're press, you understand I can't confirm or deny that. I'm working on an investigation I can't talk about. I can't tell you what this is related to but thank you for your help. Print nothing about me, or you may jeopardise this investigation.'

'I understand,' said Daniel, 'sometime do me an interview, would you? I've got to be worth that, just about being a female DI. Nice piece. Nothing gory, nothing accusatory. It's a local paper I run. People want delightful stories, cheerful stories, not a lot of blood.'

'Of course,' said Hope. 'As soon as I get a minute.' She thanked the man and put the phone down. He wasn't the first to ask her for a story about being a woman in her position.

Hope didn't see herself as being a woman. She just saw herself as being a DI.

Hope contacted the Oban police and asked them to pay a visit to the address and see if they could find David Murray. Then she spent the next hour forcing down coffee that had been made by Jackie. When Jackie came in, she stood and waited for Hope to drink it, looking for an assessment. Hope told her it was not a bad first offering, causing Jackie to smile and leave.

Hope was learning that to be in management, and certainly higher up, you had to be able to lie. The coffee was bloody awful, but it wasn't the coffee that was the important bit. It was the fact that the woman was now looking out for everyone.

Hope fielded a call from the Oban police about an hour later. There was no one at the address for David Murray, so Hope picked up the phone again, calling Daniel at the Oban newspaper.

'That was a quick return,' said Daniel. 'How can I help you?'

'The address you gave me was duff. Nobody there, never been there. It's a warehouse.'

'Okay, I'll tell you what, give me a minute. I'm going to get someone to phone you.'

'Who?' asked Hope.

'He doesn't like to say. The man does a few things for me when I need stuff investigated, but I don't want people to know about it. He's a private investigator, but I doubt he'll give you his name. I'll get him to call you. He did a bit of tracking down for me, so he may be able to give you more.'

'Okay,' said Hope. Patiently, she forced down an awful coffee for the next five minutes, and then her phone rang with an unknown number.

'Who's this?' she asked.

'I'm the man who works for Daniel at the paper. Just call me Ian.'

'You're going to help, Ian? How?'

'When Daniel was threatened, he employed me to tail Mr Murray to monitor him, in case he came back to do anything nasty.'

'He was that worried,' said Hope. 'It must have been a proper job then to be threatened like that.'

'What he described to me was that the man was wild when Daniel was rejecting his suggestion. Bit of a nutter. I followed him, but he wasn't like that. He seemed to be quite normal. Anyway, he never came back towards Daniel. He thought nothing of it. Daniel stopped paying me after a couple of days, said he didn't need it anymore.'

'You obviously found something out in that time.'

'Well, he doesn't live at the address that Daniel's got. I didn't say at the time because, well, it wasn't important. Things seemed to have blown over.'

'Where exactly does he stay?'

The man rolled off an address for Hope in the Oban area.

'That's very interesting,' she said. 'Thank you for it. Just stay out of whatever's going on down here. I warn you about that because it could be dangerous for you.'

'All right,' said the man. 'I'm pretty used to the danger. That's why I was hired.'

'No,' said Hope. 'This is dangerous, really. Stay off it.'

'Oh, there's no money involved. I won't be doing it, anyway.'

'But thank you for your time, sir,' said Hope.

She strolled over to the door, opened it, and shouted over to Susan Cunningham, 'Heading for Oban, Susan. Five minutes.'

She turned back and looked at the half-empty cup of coffee on the table. She picked it up and walked over to her window, opening the window slightly. *Yes, if you poured it down below, it would hit the grass. Nobody would know.* Hope tipped out the coffee and then heard the door open behind her. She quickly closed the window and turned to see Jackie standing there.

'Any good?' she said.

'This is top stuff, Jackie. Not a problem.'

'Do you want another?'

'Unfortunately, I've got to go to Oban.'

'I can make you one for the road.'

'Don't really like to when I'm driving.'

Hope watched the woman leave and then put the cup down, praying that Ross would be back soon, or just anyone who could make coffee.

110

Chapter 14

I t was one in the morning when Macleod got the phone call. He was still in the hospital, half dozing in a rather uncomfortable seat. He'd sent the constable home. She'd stayed with him for quite a while, but, in truth, he wanted some space. Macleod could get his own coffee if he needed it. He had eaten. He was okay.

She insisted she would come back in the morning, six o'clock. He said not to bother until eight. Where was he going to go? He was going to sit here. He might go down to the chapel on the ground floor of the hospital, maybe pray or maybe just sit in the quiet. That was the thing about the hospital corridors, sometimes they could get noisy. Although at one in the morning, they were nowhere near as noisy as during the day.

They'd finished the operation on Jane, and when he'd asked if it had gone well, the surgeon said, 'Yes. Despite some complications, but yes.' However, they wouldn't know, because of the blood loss and what her body had been through, just how she was going to be. She was far from out of the woods. The success of the operation was cold comfort, knowing that the worst part still lay ahead.

Macleod had thought about going home, but why? What would that do to calm him? Instead, he'd fret around. He'd have to go back and sort out the mess from where she'd been shot. He'd walk into a taped off area. Yes, it was his home. They'd make sure that they left it as best they could, but right now, he didn't want to walk into the nightmare of having to look at where she'd been shot.

Someone would have to run through what had happened, try to extract any information from those who've been guarding Jane about the attackers. *Thank God they missed*, he thought. *They'd missed her heart. They'd missed most of the organs. Although the bullet, or was it two—he couldn't remember—was lodged in pretty deep. Had it missed her spine? Would it affect that? They had said nothing yet, but then they didn't always. The first thing was survival. After that, it was how you looked, how you functioned. Could he handle it if she was crippled? If she was . . . Oh, I need to stop thinking like this. I need to stop thinking and start doing. What is there to do?*

Macleod stood up, walked to the lift, standing inside in the mirrored large cubicle. He felt the lift descend. As it opened at the ground floor, a porter pushing a trolley entered. As he stepped out, she gave him a smile. He tried to smile back.

She couldn't have known his situation, but they must bump into all sorts of people. People who are sad, people who are dying, people who are upbeat at success. Maybe that was a practiced smile. A smile for all that said nothing.

Macleod saw the chapel. Lights on, but no one was in there. He stepped inside, and for some reason walked to the front and sat down at what must've been an attempt at a pew. It was a series of chairs all put together. *Did they really have to make this look like a church?*

112

Of course, they'd have services here, wouldn't they, on a Sunday? What day was it?

Macleod couldn't think. He sat there, and his phone rang. If it was Hope, he didn't want to speak to her. Yes, he'd appreciated her being there, but on the phone, he'd try to talk about the case. It would all be about the case. All about what he didn't know, and he couldn't think straight on that one.

He pulled the mobile out from his pocket, looked at it. It was a man he only knew as Duncan. Duncan had been a source in the past, an old one. He was a decent, well-intentioned man, but he didn't always have a lot to share. He was homeless and generally wasn't a nuisance, keeping himself to himself. But he told Macleod a few things about the street, a few things about people's movements. Late at night, if somewhere had been broken into, Duncan was liable to have heard about it.

'Duncan, it's really not a great time.'

'But, Mr Macleod, you need to hear this.'

The other problem with Duncan was he was, for want of a better word, simple. Nice enough, absolutely not stupid, but simple. If Duncan had it in his head that something was important, it was important. He struggled to see other people's point of view.

'It's an excellent time, Mr Macleod. You need to know this.'

'Okay, Duncan,' said Macleod, 'Tell me, what is it?' Sometimes it was easier to let the man talk than to have a battle with him over it.

'Sam Jewels,' he said. 'You know Sam Jewels?'

Macleod knew Sam Jewels all right. Sam Jewels was the Inverness know-it-all. Everything on the street, Sam knew. Everything you needed to get, Sam could get to it for a price.

The more sensible criminals knew Sam, because he spoke too much, and sometimes he didn't always tell the truth. Not because he was trying to lie to you, but because he got on to many stories and exaggerated them and blew them up. He was a funny man. A character.

'Sam's being threatened, Mr Macleod. Seriously threatened.'

'If that's the case, why don't you phone 999 and let them know? You can tell them anonymously,' said Macleod. 'Duncan, you don't have to give your name. You'll be safe enough.'

'You don't understand, Mr Macleod. He's been threatened.'

'You said . . .' Macleod tried to not sound angry. 'You've already said that, and I've told you, just ring 999. It's not a good time for me, Duncan.'

'But Mr Macleod, it's by a police source. It's a police person doing it.'

A chill ran down Macleod. *No!* he thought. Macleod remembered the look on her face.

Sam Jewels lived down in the centre of town. Small flat, top one in the slightly poorer area. He had a garage close to it as well, which he operated out of, and always had a myriad of stolen goods stuck here and there. But being Sam, trying to prove they were stolen was another matter.

Macleod closed down the call after thanking Duncan and headed to the car park. He then remembered he'd been driven there. Macleod looked around for a taxi, found one, and sat in the back as he was transported to the centre of Inverness.

He was wise enough to be dropped several streets away, because he was a known face. Stumbling along, tired and weary, he got to the street that Sam Jewels lived on. He looked up at the flat, but there were no lights on. Macleod wandered on and spotted the garage a little down the street. He could see lights from within. He moved through the shadows, up close to the wall of the garage where he could listen.

'I know nothing. I know nothing. You can't do that to me. I know nothing.'

Macleod heard a thump. He leaned against the wall. Should he go in and stop her? He should. He should go in there. By rights, he should grab her and haul her out. But he was too weary. Macleod was down on his metaphorical knees. His mind couldn't think straight.

Besides, she would say no. She will say no. The trouble with a Rottweiler was that once you had upset it, got it angry, mistreated it, it did what it wanted to, and there was no control. There was no way to bring it back. He heard a yell from inside and then another one.

'Where did they source them?'

'I know nothing about sourcing things. I don't.' Thump.

'Does that vice work?' asked a furious voice.

'You want to try Jonas. You want to try Jonas.'

'Who the hell is Jonas?'

'This address. This address. He will know.'

There was silence for a while. Then a rather quiet voice said, 'That address is a cake shop. There's nobody tied to that cake shop called Jonas. I want some sensible answers, Jewels, and I want them now. That vice is coming into play, and you won't like what I'm going to put in it.'

Macleod shook his head. What was she at?

'Okay,' said the man. 'Okay. I know nothing about it. You need to . . '

There was a sound of someone being dragged. There was screaming and then a sudden protestation.

'Don't do that. You can't. Don't. I'll tell you.'

Silence, and then sobbing, and a bit more.

'It was a hush job, very hush job. Couldn't put it through any manufacturing plant. Each one's handmade. The guy who got the money for it is Italian. Alessandro. Alessandro. He's up at the University. He's an artist, creates these things.'

'How do you know that?'

'He needed some materials, materials that couldn't be traced back. Nothing illegal, just wanted all the lines removed, receipts, anything like that. It's what I do. You know that I'm not lying to you. I'm not lying to you. Don't twist that.' There was a yelp and then more tears. 'Look at me. Look what you've done to me. I haven't done that since I was a baby. Get out.'

There came a clip of heels across the garage floor. The door was opened quickly at the far side, and Macleod saw the light strobe briefly into the street. Then there were more footsteps. He walked after them, remaining about twenty yards behind. Macleod followed along three different streets until he saw a small green sports car some distance off. He whispered into the wind ahead of him,

'Clarissa, stop.'

She halted almost instantly and then turned slowly.

'Don't do this,' he said, approaching her. 'Don't. This is not a good course of action. You can't do this. This is not you. Not the way we do things. This is . . .'

'Seoras, the way we've done things, it hasn't worked. We investigated them. They cut Patterson's throat. Remember? I was there. I had to hold on to him. He bled all over me. Nearly killed your Jane. They've shot Angus. Murdered again. They're going to murder more. They didn't need to kill Patterson, didn't need to try it. We didn't bat an eyelid.

Patterson, Jane, Angus. I'm doing it for them and you. Look what they've done to you.'

'But I'm still an officer. I'm still a DCI. I'm still holding it together.'

'Who are you kidding?' fumed Clarissa.

'I passed it to Hope. I passed it to her.'

'What is she going to do, and who's she going to do it with? You're running out of people. How long until Cunningham gets taken out? How long until Hope? These people need stopped.'

'You're not some sort of thundering vigilante,' said Macleod, struggling to keep his voice down. 'We're police officers. We do our duty. You and I, we follow the law. The law is everything. If we don't have the law, we have nothing.'

'I was happy,' said Clarissa. 'I was working the art scene. People there, they're thieves. They might rough the odd person up, but you brought me into a world of nutters, psychos. How many bodies do I need to see? How can you keep going?

'Last time, they covered them with dog faeces. This time, they hang them up. They kill them in front of everyone. They kill people who don't kneel fast enough. I'm sick of it, Seoras. I'm sick of it. We picked them up afterwards, but this time, they came after my friends. This time, they're destroying you. They're destroying Ross, Angus, and Jane, and they destroyed Patterson.'

Macleod put his hand forward onto her shoulder. 'You don't think I get it? You don't think I get the pain? I don't know if she's going to survive the night, but it was important enough to come to you, because this will destroy you.'

'They did that when they cut Patterson's neck, when I had to sit there amongst the blood and keep him alive. They destroyed

117

me then.'

'No,' said Macleod. 'You're a police officer.'

'No, I'm not,' said Clarissa. 'I'm a friend. Now I know where the masks were brought from. I can get at these people, but I can't wait for procedures and . . .'

'You just intimidated him. You just . . .'

'Well, I don't want you to know what I did, but I'm good with it,' said Clarissa. 'Just let me be. Go to Jane, make sure she's fine. Make sure she heals up.'

'But you're still a police officer. You still believe in it. You know what we have to do and how we have to do it.'

'No, Seoras. I stepped away, remember? I'm not an officer anymore, but I'll sort it. I'll get you what you need. Take care.'

She turned away and strolled down the street into the little green sports car without even looking back and tore off through the night. Macleod dropped to his knees. *What do I do?* he thought. *It's all falling apart around me. What do I do?*

Chapter 15

Ross looked at the stack of papers in front of him, cutouts of crosswords, some recent. He was up to date with most things, but Angus being shot had knocked him for six. Normally, he was methodical: sit down, look at what he had to do, plan out how he was doing it, then work his way steadily through. He didn't need some moment of inspiration—he just needed to be dogged.

But now he found when he stared at certain pieces of paper or some sort of puzzle, he drifted. He went to Angus sitting in his hospital bed, back to when Angus was shot with his child somewhere in the house behind him. At first, he'd felt angry at the protection unit. They hadn't stopped the shooter. Yet, they'd taken a real battering and got back up to knock off the shooter. They'd done just enough so that the bullet ripped through Angus's shoulder and not through his heart. Logically, he should thank them, but logic didn't always cut it when emotions were this raw.

He blamed himself for being chased, for blowing his cover. He blamed himself for being a detective, for not taking the warning more seriously. It wasn't just Angus, either. Jane was fighting for her life. He remembered Macleod's face on hearing the news, seeing him at the hospital when Ross had left him to come back and look after Daniel.

Macleod was hollow. That's the only way he could think to describe him. The chief inspector was always a focused man, quiet, not a lot of mirth, but very determined. He looked rudderless suddenly. Ross had seen him through a lot of things, had been there with him when bad things had happened, but this was worse than normal. This was as bad as it had got.

The wee one was sleeping, and Ross was finally going to get a bit of time to work his way through some of the crosswords. He wouldn't have been bothered, but Macleod had asked Ross. Really, he deserved the time to sort his family out, but Macleod had asked. And if Macleod could ask when he was sitting awaiting news about his partner's potential fight for life, then Ross could make the effort. If Hope had asked, well, that would've been different.

Ross had fielded a phone call from Clarissa.

'Als,' she'd said. Even now she couldn't call him by his proper name. 'Are you okay? Do you need anything, Als?'

All that Ross needed was an occasional babysitter while he went up to see Angus, and he was thinking he was going to take Daniel with him, anyway. If he was looking at a potential babysitter, Clarissa would not be one of those people. She wouldn't have had the patience for it.

But she'd sounded different. She'd sounded more than grumpy. Angry, truly angry. It was a voice that gave Ross concern.

Ross looked down at the crossword from the Oban paper and filled in the last of the clues. Messages were probably still being passed. In fact, he knew they would be, but the coding must have been slightly different because on this one, it made no sense. Not the old method he'd been using. The cipher was different.

Ross looked at the crossword and tried to bring himself back to the moment. He sought his happy place, that place where he just stared and letters moved, patterns emerged. Slowly, he took a breath. He closed his eyes and then slowly opened them, letting them wander across the letters.

They picked out pieces here and there, moving them round and then saw if they sat well. Usually, they didn't. Usually, there was a load of nonsense, but sometimes it worked for him. He opened the eyes, letting them drift. He saw the word *hotel* spelled out.

Okay, so we're five along this time, and we're coming down and across. Ross wrote a quick note of the cipher he thought he was using. Now he followed it, *Hotel. Bradshaw's.* That was a relatively new building on the edge of Inverness. He scanned and saw the word Inverness. *Who is it? Who is it?* he thought.

Ross worked backwards through the puzzle, seeing where the first letters were coming from now. *Jones. Jones, who was Jones?* He typed Jones into Google. Then he typed Money, Finance.

Jones Pensions was a pensions company, or was it more of a hedge fund? Ross wasn't sure, but it certainly looked like something. He clicked to their website. There was a company meeting, a getting together. They were bringing all the staff together.

'Oh, hell,' said Ross. He continued to work through and found the date. *Today? Today!* He reached for the phone.

'This is Macleod. What's the matter?'

The boss must have been sleeping, Ross thought. He sounded tired. 'Did I wake you?'

'Yes, you did. I was up part of the night, Alan. I was . . .'

'How is she?'

'Just the same. Just the same.'

'Look, I've been going through crosswords like you've asked. I've got a match. Today. Jones Pensions. The company is at Bradshaw's Hotel for a conference. Do you want me to call Hope as well?'

'Hope's headed off to Oban,' said Macleod. 'Taken Cunningham with her. No, I'll go. I'll get this.'

'I can get the constables to go, get the Desk Sergeant to . . .'

'No. No, I'll go,' said Macleod.

'I'll come if you need me.'

'You've got the wee one. You've got no cover. Stay at home. No, it's fine. It's fine, Ross. Good work though. Good work. I'll get on it.'

* * *

Macleod hauled himself up off the plastic seating in the hospital. He swung to his feet. *How long had he been asleep? Maybe four, five hours?*

He tore off down the stairs, picking up his mobile phone again and calling the Desk Sergeant. He asked for help to send as many cars as possible out towards Bradshaw's Hotel. This wasn't about catching people in the act. This was about protection, safety, and clearing that hotel.

Macleod made it out to the car park and then realised, once again, he didn't have his car. Should he run over to the station, grab it from there? Instead, he hailed a taxi.

'The Bradshaw's Hotel,' he said. 'Fast as you can.' He pulled his warrant card out. 'We need to get there as fast as you can.'

The taxi left the hospital, and as it went out onto the road, it was suddenly engulfed by other police cars racing past it, sirens blaring. The drive was less than ten minutes. When the taxi driver pulled up, Macleod could see several police cars already there, constables rushing in towards the hotel.

Macleod climbed out, threw the driver some notes, and marched over towards the hotel. It was a reasonably minor affair, quite small for a conference venue, but that didn't matter. Ross had done the numbers, and they had ended up there. Macleod entered the hotel. He saw two police officers heavily engaged with the receptionist. He strolled over towards them.

'What are we doing? Clear it. Clear everything. No risks.'

'Morning, sir. I'm afraid that won't be necessary.'

'What do you mean not necessary?' asked Macleod. 'I said clear the place.'

'You also said there was a conference on, there's not.'

'Jones Pension Company,' said Macleod. 'Here at Bradshaw's Hotel. It said here today.'

'No,' said the receptionist. 'You're six months early.' Macleod froze. 'They booked for six months' time. Sorry, but I don't know what's going on, but there's nothing happening here today,' said the receptionist.

Macleod stopped for a moment. He turned and walked to the door and looked out at the countryside beyond him. *What were these people at?* he thought. They sent a message out through the Oban paper. Are they just checking? Are they just checking to see what . . . He grabbed his phone.

'This is Hope.'

'Hope, it's Seoras. David Moore, find him now. Find him now because I think he's been compromised.'

'What do you mean?' asked Hope.

'Ross found a message in the Oban letter, sent me over to

Bradshaw's Hotel to cover a meeting of the Jones Pensions Company. It's not happening today. It's happening in six months. They're checking and I've just turned up with police cars. They'll know he's been compromised. Whatever he's doing is compromised. You know what they'll do.'

'On it, Seoras, on it.'

* * *

Susan Cunningham looked over at Hope. The woman had answered the phone quickly, and then her face had become deeply agitated.

'David Moore's cover's been blown,' said Hope. 'We need to find him. We need to find him quick.'

'Well, we don't know what he works at,' said Susan.

'We go to his address. We need to go to his address.'

The two women took off in the car, arriving at the address for David Moore, which was a small house near an industrial estate. It looked pretty run down. Hope arrived, banging loudly on the door.

'This is the police. We believe your life's in danger, Mr. Moore. Open up. Open up.' She continued banging on it until a neighbour appeared over a small fence between the houses.

'Did you say you're the police?' It was an old woman. 'Because you'll not find him here. He goes out for his walk. Wanders down to the piers. He likes to go down, see where the ferry runs across, walk down by the RNLI station. Got the big ferries coming in too. That's where he'll be, down at Oban pier.'

'Thank you,' said Hope, and turned, telling Susan, 'Do not hold back on the speed to get there.'

124

They raced through the traffic, which wasn't that busy. They arrived at the pier, stopped the car, and walked through an opening to get onto the different piers. Hope could see someone at the far end of one and several people approaching him. The first man was wearing a jacket and looked like he was out for a walk. As for the others, Hope could see grey habits.

'There, Susan, there. Come on.'

She took off with Cunningham in her wake. Hope approached the end of the pier towards who she thought was David Moore being attacked by three men. The men had masks on, and when Hope ran up behind them, she drove a fist into the back of one. There was a cry of pain before the second one turned to face her.

Cunningham jumped on the third, but he was strong and knocked her off. Hope had her attacker down to the ground and was about to handcuff him when she felt a blow to the back of the head. She stumbled towards the ground but managed to roll away. Hope stood up and took another attacker head on, driving her knee up into his midriff, spinning him round, and then throwing him to the ground.

She kicked out at the second one approaching her and dived on the first, placing handcuffs on him. He was face down, and Hope only just stood back up before she was attacked again. She put up a blocking hand but took a blow to the face and then another couple to her midriff. She was pushed backwards and clattered into Cunningham. Together, the two of them fell to the floor and received a couple of kicks.

Hope stood up at the edge of the pier boards. She spun and grabbed Cunningham's attacker, throwing him behind her where he tumbled into the man that had gone to the ground.

The two men stumbled over each other, then one produced a knife racing at Hope with it. He slashed forward as she stepped to one side, grabbed his wrist, and snapped it hard. He cried out in pain, but the other man kicked her, causing her to drop slightly.

'Come on, we need to get the hell out of here.'

She saw them run to their other colleague, who was driving himself back up onto his feet, even though he was still handcuffed from behind.

'Get him. Don't let them go,' Hope cried out to Cunningham. Then something else caught her eye. David Moore had stood up. He didn't look relieved. Instead, he walked calmly and jumped off the pier into the water.

'Susan, back, get back here. He's just gone in.'

'What? What do you mean?'

'He's just thrown himself into the water. Get the Coastguard. Get the authorities. I'm going in after him.'

Susan Cunningham stood in the moment of shock. Over her shoulder, three men in masks were running in front of her. Her boss was diving off the pier into the cold water of the harbour. She picked up her phone, and dialled 999. As she relayed the details and the help she required, part of her mind was trying to work out why David Moore would suddenly jump into the water. As she did so, she wandered over to the edge of the pier and saw a redhead coming up to look at her.

'Can't see him, diving for him.'

Hope disappeared back under the surface. Cunningham stood and watched because there seemed so little else she could do.

Chapter 16

Ross trundled upstairs in his house and placed his wee one into the small bed. It had done Angus good to see him. Both of them. It had done Ross good, too. Angus was awake. He was talking. He was okay. His worst problem was he was bothered by the policeman on the door of the hospital room. Macleod had asked for one to be put there just in case somebody came back to finish the job.

Macleod hadn't been there. He'd taken off after Ross had passed on the information. He hadn't returned during Ross's visit. Ross wandered back down the stairs of the house, made his way into the kitchen and put on a coffee. He watched as the filter machine dripped what looked like dark and muddy brown liquid into a small flask. It was insulated, and the coffee in it would stay warm for the next four or five hours.

Angus had bought it. Previously, Ross always had a normal filter machine with the glass jug at the bottom, but the coffee was always cold after an hour. Angus had one now where the coffee could sit for three or four hours and still be piping hot when it came into your cup. It was just one of the many things around the house that Angus had done. That's what he was good at, little touches. Ross always appreciated little touches.

He glanced down at the phone that he'd just brought out of his pocket. He saw a message from Macleod detailing everything he knew about a David Murray, a man who had been putting crosswords into one of the Oban papers. That was the one that Ross had picked up that day and then solved and passed to Macleod. Now, Macleod was asking him to look deeper into Murray.

Believing there was enough liquid in the collecting flask, Ross poured some into a cup. He put the vessel back underneath to collect the remaining liquid yet to drop. Once settled down in front of his computer, he typed in David Murray, and he typed in finance and then pensions. At first, most of the links didn't seem to show anything, but one was linked through to a Twitter tweet, a run about financial irregularity with a small link from it.

Ross clicked through on the link and found a small article in a rather unknown paper. There was a photograph of David Murray. Ross sat and read the article. Murray's father had pension money tucked away with his job, but the pension had collapsed. The article didn't say why but blamed the number of parental firms.

Ross noted down the dates and the times, and any other information he could. Now he looked into public records and financial accounts. It wasn't long before a red flag had been put up. He could see that the pension company had allowed pension money to be used to bolster other companies in the group, instead of paying out. There'd been a reprimand, but nothing had been proven. The company was still trading.

Ross went back to the original links and decided to see if he could find any more tweets about what had gone on. He found one from David Murray, showing a picture of his father.

'They killed him,' he tweeted. 'They killed him. Something must be done.'

Ross compiled everything together to send off in an email to Macleod and Hope, but as he was about to push send, they came a knock at the front door. There were still two police officers out there, but given what had happened before, Ross went over to the window from which he could see the front door. A man stood there in a long raincoat and he recognised his boss. Quickly, Ross opened the door. 'How is she?'

'I wish people would stop asking me that. She's the bloody same.'

Oh-Oh, thought Ross. *He actually swore.*

'Sorry,' he said. 'Come through, the wee one's asleep. In fact, I've just found out some stuff for you.'

'Murray ran,' said Macleod suddenly.

'What do you mean?' asked Ross.

'Exactly what I say. You gave me that note for the hotel today. I chased it, nobody was there. They were checking whether their code had been cracked. Somebody was there and a group of them went to meet Murray, obviously to finish him, but Hope and Susan got there. However, once they chased off those attacking Murray, Murray jumped into the water.

'A suicide.'

'Well, a failed suicide thankfully,' said Macleod. 'Hope pulled him out of the water. He's the only line we've got now.'

'Maybe, but I also know why he is doing it, so he might not be the only line.'

Ross explained to Macleod about David Murray's father, about the pension money. He then explained how he could now search around that company, who had pensions, for who could be involved. They could then send uniform out to speak to them, because it may have been a large number.

'Come in and sit down,' said Ross. 'Are you heading back up to the hospital?'

'They'll phone me if something happens,' said Macleod. 'They'll phone me. I've got to get on with this.'

'You've got to sit down,' said Ross. 'You are exhausted. When was the last sleep you got?'

'I got four, maybe five hours before we had to run out to Bradshaw's. I haven't been back to the house either.'

'No, you don't look your usual crisp self,' said Ross. 'You should let somebody else take this over.'

'Who? Hope is off exploring. We need somebody back at the base here. If Clarissa was here, if she hadn't gone off and . . .'

'Hadn't gone off what?'

Macleod looked down at the table. 'You can't breathe a word of this.'

'That's not like you. You know I wouldn't.'

'No, but you have to understand she's . . .'

'She's what? She rang me—asked how Angus was.'

'She's gone to sort this out on her own. The last thing she told me was she was no police officer, but she's gone to sort it out on her own. She went to see Sam Jewels, put the squeeze on him, but a rough version of the squeeze. She's free-ranging, Ross. I don't need this. She's free-ranging. We can't be emotional. We can't react like that.'

'How the hell do you expect people to react?' said Ross suddenly. 'What do you expect? They nearly blew Angus away. They've taken down Jane. We can't get near them at the moment. The woman's just out there doing everything she can to end this. Where does this go? You tell me that.' Macleod looked up and saw Ross's clenched fist. 'If I hadn't had the wee one, I'd join her. We need to fight back. We need to get in on them.'

'We follow the law. We always follow the law, Ross. You can't just . . .'

'Well, they don't, do they? They know how to play this. That's part of the problem. They're a step ahead. They didn't follow the law when they cut Patterson's throat. They didn't follow the law when they shot Jane. If I had them here for what they did to my Angus . . .'

'I know you're angry. I know you're—'

'No, I'm angry,' said Ross. He turned and kicked the chair. It slid across the kitchen floor, banging off a cupboard. 'The wee guy is asleep upstairs. They could have taken him. This feels more like a war, sir,' spat Ross.

'I'll go,' said Macleod, 'before you say something I can't be a part of.'

'I have dug into the records for you,' said Ross, 'and I will keep doing it. You don't have to worry about me freelancing. I've got to stay here. I have people to look after. Clarissa doesn't. That's why she's gone. That's why she's doing it. You realise we're her family, don't you?'

'Still doesn't give us the right.'

'If we can end this, of course, it gives us the right.' Ross poured a cup of coffee into a cup. He placed it in front of Macleod. 'You need to sleep,' said Ross, gently. 'You need . . .'

'I need Jane to be okay because if she's not, I may charge down that route Clarissa is on, and I can't do that.'

There was a silence in the kitchen, broken only by the occasional sputter of the filter in the coffee machine. There was no noise from upstairs. Outside, the street was fairly quiet.

The two men sat without looking at each other before Macleod gently offered, 'Try to find some more of those companies that were involved in the pension scandal. This is what it's all about this time. It's all about financial irregularity. We need to deal with it. We need to find it. Get onto the Ombudsman or people in the city, whatever. Expand out from Murray's account on Twitter or whatever else he's on. We need to keep working hard on this. We need to keep pushing, Ross. It'll come, trust me.'

'But it might come too late for people,' Ross whispered. 'I'm not used to them taking potshots at us. Get warded off, yes. But not like this. This isn't the way they do it. This is not criminal behaviour.'

'No, it's more like terrorism,' said Macleod. 'But there's an undercurrent. There's somebody at the core of this. I can feel it. Somebody and he's got an issue with me.'

'What makes you think that? He shot Angus, as well as Jane. It wasn't just you. I was mentioned.'

'The first part of all of this, the Stornoway connection. They said that something was wrong over there. I went to Ross; I went to McNeil and the others. They all said nothing. They all said that there was one issue. We went there and dealt with that. That wasn't the issue that's being looked into. It isn't the one that's being brought to the fore by these people.'

'You worked there though,' said Ross. 'And I know you. You wouldn't have stood for that.'

'You all say you know me, but you see the finished product. Back then, I wasn't as sharp. I wasn't as shrewd. I was still decent. I still believed in the law, Ross. I still would've held up any of the officers that broke it in that way. But could something have happened? I just didn't see it. But McNeil was a decent man. He was a church elder. Yes, he was officious, sexist, in a lot of ways, but times were sexist then. A woman's place back in the kitchen. Woman's place beside her man, behind their man. That's what it was in those days. It was normal. To abuse, that wasn't. It still would've been pulled up. Especially if it was anything to do with youngsters.'

'Then I don't get why he's coming at you. You spoke to all of them. They said nothing. They said that there was no problem. Everyone that was in Stornoway, nobody could recall anything. They can't all be corrupt. Surely,' said Ross.

'They spoke to me face to face. You would hope not, but why pull them all out? Why? This isn't just to annoy me. If it was just to annoy us, why didn't things go deeper with Hope or with you? Why is it not more out front?'

'Maybe they didn't have the ability then. They seem to have grown. There seem to be more people involved now.'

'And the aim, or rather the cause, has changed,' said Macleod. 'It's become general. It helps to take people on board but he seems much more prepared to lose people. I think the mind must have gone because we didn't nip him in the bud. He thought he can do more. We may have lost it badly this time, Ross. We may have.'

'Stop it,' said Ross suddenly. 'You need to get back up to it. You need to, oh, I don't know,' said Ross. 'I don't know what you need. You've come in here, you've moped, you've pushed me to do this. Just get out for a bit and let Hope run it.'

'I can't leave her to do that. Do you understand? Too many people coming and we don't know. You're not there to pick up the loose ends, either.'

'Then get someone who can,' said Ross. 'I'll work. I'll chase things from here, but you need to do what I did and put your

133

family first. Screw the investigation. Just get back to that hospital with Jane.'

Macleod stood up, leaving a half-empty cup of coffee. As he walked through the front door, he turned back to Ross.

'Companies involved. Get me names of companies involved in these pension irregularities. We'll go from there.'

Chapter 17

H ope McGrath had showered and stepped out to a welcome towel and begun to dry herself down. As she stood in the cubicle, she heard movement outside in the women's changing area.

'Hello.'

'I don't want to rush you,' said Susan Cunningham suddenly. 'But I just had a call from Ross. Seems the big boss is not faring so well. He said he's heard him complaining about Clarissa.'

'What about her?' asked Hope, drying her hair.

'It seems she's gone rogue,' said Susan.

Hope clicked the lock on the door of the cubicle. About to step out, she suddenly stopped herself, grabbed the towel, and wrapped it round her. She then stood out and looked over at Cuningham. 'What do you mean, rogue?'

'According to Ross, Macleod said that she'd gone to see somebody called Sam Jewels.'

'Sam Jewels,' said Hope. 'Bit of a mouth. He always knows what's going on in Inverness. Nothing much wrong with that. That's not going rogue.'

'Ross said that Macleod said she'd used undue force.'

'Okay,' said Hope. She turned away, back into the cubicle,

135

closed it, and began drying herself again.

'Is that it?' asked Cunningham. 'Is that all I get?'

'What do you want?' asked Hope.

'Urquhart. Could she screw this whole investigation up?'

Hope went silent. Macleod had brought Clarissa in, and she was good for the team, kept them on their toes, but she was hot-headed and she could fly off the handle. *Could she bring this investigation down? Could she?*

Hope unlocked the door again and leaned out, holding the towel over herself. 'Frankly, yes, she could.'

'Then we need to do something about her. We need to go get her stopped.'

'Give me a minute,' said Hope. She stepped back inside the cubicle, dried herself, threw on her pants and a T-shirt, and stepped outside again into the women's changing area. 'Sit down, Cunningham.'

'Cunningham, is it?'

'You need to understand something about Clarissa. If Macleod's gone there, if he's heard stuff, and he's not bringing her in, he's not doing it out of loyalty. He's not doing it because he doesn't want to book her, he doesn't want to have her charged, or he doesn't want to sully the name of the rest of us. Seoras doesn't work that way. This may be hard to understand, but there's a part of him believes this is how we're going to bust this case. I think he would have sent her in hard-nosed, not like this, not outside the law, but he would have sent her in hard to shake things up. If she'd still been with us.'

'But she's not,' said Cunningham.

'No, she's not, but maybe that makes it easier.'

'Don't make it right though, does it?'

'No, it doesn't, but think about it; our every move is being watched. We've just had two people shot, two loved ones. John's even been brought into this, a body dumped in the back of one of his hire cars. You haven't because they don't know you yet. You've come into the investigation later. Nobody from Patterson's family was ever touched, although he obviously was badly hurt in the line of duty.

'They haven't just gone and committed their acts against these ministers and now these corporations, they've come at us. It's subtle. It's done in a way that you could say that we've been thrown off the scent. No, they're coming for us and I think coming for Macleod. I think they're coming for the boss. This whole talk of distraction, of being sent cards about the killings of the ministers as a way of distracting us from things. I don't believe it.

'The nature of what these people are about, unearthing past indiscretions or outright blatant breaches of trust. You don't do that because it seems like a good idea to clear up. If you think it's a good idea simply to clear them up, you organise a campaign, you go on telly. No, these guys are out to exact revenge and that means . . .'

'They're coming for one of us about something, something in the past.'

'Exactly,' said Hope. 'Only, this is DCI Seoras Macleod. Seoras has unearthed nasty stuff about other officers. He has ripped his DCIs apart for what they were doing. Seoras holds a standard higher than most and yet he's happy to let Clarissa go off half-cocked. He thinks that's how we're going to get to the truth. He doesn't know what it is they're coming after him for and he thinks they're coming after him.'

'Why?' asked Susan.

'He hasn't asked me about any indiscretions I've had in the

past. He hasn't asked me if I've been involved in any cover-ups. Seoras hasn't spoken to Ross; he hasn't spoken to Clarissa about that. He was the only one among us who received the card. He is convinced they're coming for him, and I tell you now. If they're coming for him, we will fight back with everything we've got and if that means we have to go on the outside, we'll do it, but he's getting Clarissa to do it.'

'You mean it's all been a setup, Clarissa leaving? Okay. That doesn't ring true. She got married as well.'

'No setup. He didn't plan it that way. When she left and then she just got angry, she's decided to end this. Seoras has just gone with it. He's seen it as the way to do it. People think Seoras rules the roost, and he just picks what to do. Well, he picks what to do after seeing what everyone else is offering. He comes to you and learns from you. That's why he's so good.

'He's not an island, unless someone's come for him. He knows that this is Clarissa's way of helping. She's good on the outside. She's used to working alone from her art-world days and she knows how to handle people. Trust me, if he hadn't wanted her to do this, he'd have pulled her in. At the moment, he's all over the place, Susan, but you're part of the team. So, let's get back to what we need to do. Do our job, like Clarissa, do what we need to do.'

Hope went back to change further and when she came out, Susan Cunningham was standing, brushing her hair.

'It helps you think, doesn't it?'

'What,' said Susan.

'It helps you think. I sit and brush my hair even when it doesn't need brushed when I need to ponder what to do. You're undecided. You're thinking, should I go to someone with this?'

'My senior officer just said it's okay to let someone else run rogue.'

'You call it, Susan. Want to run it in? I'll come with you. We'll go see the Assistant Chief Constable. We'll go see Seoras; we'll go tell him. I'll call him now. I don't want to be sitting worrying if I have to keep things from you. Call it now. Please, just stop brushing your hair.'

Hope could see her hands trembling. 'Remember Patterson and what they've just done to our colleagues and partners.'

Cunningham grabbed her hair, and put it up in a ponytail. Hope's was already fixed. 'Let's go', Hope said.

'Just like that? Just like that? You aren't even asking me what my decision is.'

'You just tied your ponytail up so you're ready for duty. Seoras said you were like me. Not exactly the same, but very like me.'

'He was right. Let's get to work.'

Five minutes later, both women were sitting opposite David Murray. He refused to look at them. Hope sat back, allowing Susan to question him.

Susan ran through the time on the pier. She ran through what he'd been doing before with the crosswords, but he said nothing. Hope was armed with something else and she showed Murray the note sent through from Ross. It told of the pension money and the company screwing his father over and ended with the suicide that Murry's father committed. After Susan had exhausted her questions, Hope stood up, turned her back on Murray, and pretended to walk out of the room.

'Well, that's it, David. That's your struggle done. You'd like to avenge your father, but it didn't happen. You'd like to have it known he was forced into suicide, but that won't happen. Everyone will remember him as a man who just couldn't take it. Everyone will remember him as . . .'

'Don't you damn well say that, you lying bitch!'

Hope turned on her heel. 'Liar, am I? Hi. Whatever happened to him, the man committed suicide because he couldn't cope with his financial troubles.'

'Financial troubles those bastards put him in. That's why they have to pay.'

'Who has to pay? You tell me who has to pay because I don't see anyone out there,' said Hope. 'I don't see any evidence. I see nothing.'

'You people only see what you want to see.' He folded his arms and looked down at the table in front of him.

'The world sees a suicide, see's somebody that couldn't handle it. They'll see his son, the man who talked about how his father wasn't this, wasn't that, but he couldn't even open his mouth while with the police to explain to them what's going on. Who couldn't?'

'I'm not running in people I'm working with.'

'You could have gone for a petition,' said Hope. 'You could have petitioned. Got records published. You could have . . .'

'And what would that do? It will not happen, will it? These people are too powerful. Way too powerful.'

'Who's too powerful?' said Hope. 'Who? Because now, all I see is a weakling on the other side who can't even call out the names of the companies you accuse?'

'There was Bradley finance,' said Murray quietly. 'They did it at Cora too, but they're one of many. Wasn't only my father who suffered.'

'That seems small to me. Seems small fry. Oh, here's a name. Talk out, toss out these finance people. Just blame the people with the money.'

'You look at Cora,' he said, 'Cora people were at it. But it all got passed away. It all got pushed aside. Couldn't prove this. Couldn't show that. Damn accountants—can't do anything against them.'

'No, but *their* accountants must have been able to, don't you think?'

'Lynch's firm. Lynch's firm's taken out as well. They're the problem.'

'When will you hit them? When will you hit them, David?'

He halted and laughed. 'We'll hit them. We'll hit them soon enough,' he said. 'Who though? Who?' He folded his arms, looked over at Hope. 'You're good,' he said. 'You're good. Get me angry. Get me one thing to tell you all about it. Well, I've told you enough. You aren't getting any more out of me. I will not drop anyone in it. I'd rather die than drop them in it. You shouldn't have saved me. You know that?'

'That's not my opinion,' said Hope, 'But thank you for the information. Terminate the interview.'

Hope walked outside, picked up her phone and contacted Ross.

'We got Bradley Finance, Cora, Lynch accountants. David Murray's giving them all up as being part of who was involved in the irregularities around his father's pensions account. Get into them, Ross. He said they were going to hurt them soon.'

'And they will do,' said Ross. 'Got the paper from Fort William, except they're running a more complicated cypher. But I've got numbers. I've got numbers that show it's tomorrow. I'm going to see where these companies are and what they're doing.'

'Good,' said Hope, 'let me know when. I'll head back. Keep Murray under lock and key.'

Susan Cunningham caught up with Hope. She went into the little canteen at the police station.

'You certainly riled him up.'

'I did, and you played your part well. You gave him the standard questions. He wasn't ready for me. It's just funny doing it.'

'Why?' asked Susan.

'Because I was doing Seoras's part today. He usually lets me drift in there, especially with men. Men automatically want to look at the woman, especially if it's Seoras as the other choice. It's not just about looks though, though a large part of it is. Some of it's about warmth, thinking they'll get a better response from a female.'

'But he had two females there.'

'He was very relaxed at the start. He said nothing, and he kept his eyes on both of us until I stood up. That's why I stood up. That's why I turned and I went angry at him. I twisted his image of me around, and it caught him off guard. Three names. Ross has got dates. We could be on the move quickly, so if you're having coffee, have it quick. I think we're back to Inverness.'

Chapter 18

I had rained heavily at first and she'd been standing outside in it. It had been necessary not to leave the little green sports car close to the scene. The scene in question was a flat at the top of a selection of dwellings made of former houses in the old part of Inverness. The time was one in the morning and Clarissa stood under an umbrella.

However, her trews were completely soaked, the rain bouncing hard off the pavement. She felt warm on her top half with a tartan shawl wrapped tight around her.

She had mixed feelings about what she was doing. Her husband had called several times on the phone asking where she was. They hadn't been married that long, barely at all, and already she was running off to do something without his knowledge.

That was essential. He couldn't be a part of this. He couldn't know what activities she was undertaking or where she was. However, the text she sent him, 'Trust me, I'm fine. I will be back,' was hardly substantial. She was banking on a lot of trust amongst two people who hadn't known each other that long.

The wind picked up as the rain died down and Clarissa had to collapse the umbrella before it blew in on itself. The light in the top flat was still on, but rather than break in, she was hoping for one of the other flat owners to return. She'd been waiting now for an hour and a half, and with the umbrella down, even the shawl was feeling heavy from the rain.

It was a blonde-haired girl with some bloke being dragged behind her. *Young love*, thought Clarissa, *or maybe it was one of those drunken ones, off to the club. Smashed out of your brain. Pick up whatever you find, back for a night of alcohol-forgotten sex, and questioning eyes in the morning thinking, 'Who on earth is that?'*

There had been times, she thought, but those times were a long time ago. She should be waking up with a man whose arms seemed to encompass her without even trying, but this was important. Someone was coming for the team. Someone was coming for Macleod, she could tell.

Clarissa needed to get to the source, needed to find out who this was, and bring them down. She was no longer within the law, no longer having to set the example of not putting the third boot in, stopping only after the two times. Clarissa smiled to herself. She'd have to be careful, though. These people were killers, though she didn't believe this person was.

The young couple opened the door and stood in the doorway for a moment, kissing. Then she hauled the man through the door, slowly closing the door behind him. Clarissa walked forward, threw a stick into the gap, and watched as the door almost shut. It was being held open ever so slightly by the impromptu stick she'd picked up.

Once the couple had finally got over crawling all over themselves, and gone inside their flat, Clarissa opened the door. She kicked the stick away and closed it behind her.

The staircase was lit. Incredibly bright after her eyes had

been peering through the gloom outside, she took a moment as she walked up to allow them to adjust. The light had still been on in the top flat.

Clarissa walked quietly up the stairs, keeping to one side, using her tiptoes on each flight. It meant her knees ached more as she walked, but she wanted to be quiet, wanted there to be no chance that anybody had seen her go up.

There were no security cameras in these old flats. They weren't built with the wide sweeping staircases that modern-day ones had. You couldn't get a wardrobe up here. Not unless you employed those special blokes who knew how to do it, the ones that seemed to bend furniture around any corners. These were the old staircases that could creak and moan if you weren't careful. Otherwise, you were unseen.

Clarissa reached the top floor and saw the single door leading to the flat at the top. She marched up to it and gently, but with intent, rapped the door with her knuckles. Hearing movement, she smiled to herself as the door cracked. She could see the chain that was there preventing the door from opening fully, and a pair of eyes appeared around the edge.

'What the hell do you want?'

'I've come about the order,' she said.

'What order?'

'The rest of the masks.' It was a punt. It might be a good one.

'I'm only half a day late. I said they'd be ready. Not my fault they wanted to push up the timescale.'

'I'm here to discuss some things. Let me in, please.'

'But you don't come to me. We know where the delivery point is. I'll deliver them there.'

'You wouldn't like another visit. There'll be more of them. You're lucky you're getting the old woman first.'

The man peered at her. Then she heard the snib being unlocked, and the door opened.

'Come on in,' he said. 'If that's the way it is, at least we can talk about it civilly.' She heard the door close behind her. The snib being put on and more locks being introduced.

'I take it you have some examples here. They want me to look at the workmanship.'

'They've not complained before. Everything's been fine. It's been on time. Untraceable, too.'

'Oh, we have got no complaints. We just like to keep a check,' said Clarissa.

She strolled into what looked like a mess of a room. Clearly, at one end there was a work area, but boxes and other pieces had been stashed in the corner and spilled out across the floor. She believed there was some sort of brown carpet underneath, but it was difficult to make out.

'Do you want a drink?' asked the man.

'No, I'm not here to socialise,' said Clarissa. 'I'm here to look at the merchandise. Now, let me have a look.'

'They didn't say before about you coming,' said the man, as he made his way over to a box and reached inside. He pulled out a mask, handing it to Clarissa. 'You can try that.'

Clarissa was wearing gloves, so she picked up the mask, put it in front of her face, making sure it didn't touch any part of her other than the gloved hand.

'They look good,' she said. 'How many have you got for him?'

'Enough. The ones they asked, they're difficult to make. Solid. They won't move when you fight. They'll fit in nicely with the habit.'

'Good,' said Clarissa.

'Why has he sent you?' asked the man. Clarissa walked

146

over to the window facing herself, just behind the curtain, but looking out into the street below, no one was about. With a glance, she looked at the mirror on the wall and could see the man in it. He looked nervous.

'Sometimes we need to check up. You may be aware there's been a bit of commotion. You may have seen things in the news.'

The man looked really nervous now. 'No. No, I just keep my head down, do my job. That's all. That's all I need to do. You keep paying me the money. They're still leaving it at the same drop-off point, aren't they?'

'That's not my concern,' said Clarissa. 'Someone else looks after that bit once the masks have arrived. I'm what you might call quality control. Nothing more, nothing less.'

'But the drop point is still the same?' asked the man.

'Quality control,' said Clarissa. 'We make sure we don't all know things. We don't all know what's going on. If any of us get caught, we can't tell the entire story. We don't all have your name, but I do,' said Clarissa.

'How did you get in? That door locks down there, you can't just override it. You can't.'

'But you can follow someone in,' said Clarissa. 'You're not the most well-protected.'

'You haven't used a code word yet,' said the man. 'Why not? They said everybody would use the code word. The code word was important. The code word was everything. Why haven't you used the code word?'

'Give it time,' she said. 'Not all of us use it straight away, and we're not meant to say it out loud, are we?'

'No,' said the man, but Clarissa caught him in the mirror, seeing him quietly step across the room and pick up a phone out of his cradle. She turned, walked across, seeing his wide eyes staring at her.

'What?' he asked. She reached forward, grabbed the phone, and then his hand, placing the hand on the cradle before ramming the phone down on it. 'Going to call on me, were you?'

The man yelled, but only briefly before Clarissa's other hand shot over his mouth. She stamped hard on his foot and then kneed him in the groin. He doubled over, but she held him by the hair, wheeled him round and threw him towards the sofa. He collapsed down on top of it. Clarissa picked up her umbrella where she'd left it, lying against the chair. She pointed the tip at the man's stomach, driving it hard in.

'First, shut up. If you speak again without being asked, I will press this tip of the umbrella out through your back into the sofa. My name is not important and who I represent is unimportant. What is important is that you tell me everything you know about making these masks.'

Terror shot through the man's face. He went to speak then didn't, choking on words, finding them difficult to produce to satisfy Clarissa, but also those who had put him to this.

'There's no middle ground here,' she said. 'You will tell me everything.'

'Who are you?' he said. Clarissa drove the point of the umbrella into his stomach hard before releasing it. 'I didn't ask you that,' she said, 'I want to know who's giving you these.'

'The job,' he said. 'I don't know who is the job. I have seen no one. That's why I'm surprised you were here.'

'So how do you communicate?' asked Clarissa.

'Drop sequence. It's all by drop sequence. We have bins we leave things in. The orders come through. I drop the masks at a certain place. Money gets left in another. I never see them. Never have seen them.'

'When are these masks being delivered? The next day or two?'

'Yes,' he said, 'The next day or two. I've got more to do.'

'That's good,' she said. 'That's good, because I need to know where and when.'

You've got to be crazy,' said the man, 'they'll kill you. They'll kill me. You've seen what they do on the television. They hung those people. They hung them out at that hotel.'

'You haven't seen what I can do. I'll hang you here. I'll make your life a misery for the next week before I get rid of you. Trust me,' said Clarissa. She stamped hard on the man's foot. There was a crunch. A toe may have broken, she wasn't sure, but the man doubled over in pain. He was desperately trying to stop from crying out.

'Good. You're learning,' said Clarissa. 'How many more have you got to make? Because clearly, you're up to working through the night.'

'I've got another four to finish. When I do them, I have to message them for a drop point.'

'You'll be finishing them then tonight, with a message in the morning.'

'They'll kill me.'

'You'll have a fair chance to get away. I won't dump you into them. I'll give you a chance to run.'

The man looked at her wide-eyed. 'Why are you doing this? You must be, what? Seventy?'

Clarissa lifted the point and drove it into the man's groin. As he doubled over, she stepped back.

'That's just plain rude,' she said. 'I don't mind when we're

149

doing business, but if you're going to be rude about it, I'll hurt you properly.'

'Don't. Damn, that hurts.' The man could barely speak.

'Have you got to be anywhere else? Is there anybody that will miss you if you're not about for the next two days?'

The man shook his head. He looked up at her now, tears in his eyes. Maybe she'd been a touch vicious with that, but frankly, after what had happened, she couldn't care less. Inside, she was happy. She had a way in, a way to find them. It wouldn't be easy, it really wouldn't, and she'd be spending the night with this idiot.

'What do you want me to do?' asked the man.

'You'll get back over there and you'll finish those masks. We'll then have a sleep, and tomorrow, you'll go out and drop the message, and then we'll work from there. At no point will you betray me, because I'll give you up to them instantly. They'll kill you. If you run with me, we'll get to a point where I'm happy that you've given me all you can, and you can run. You can run from this country as fast as you want. I think that's a fair deal in the context.'

The man looked at her, clearly not believing so.

'You make masks for killers. You know they kill. As a concerned relative, don't even try to pretend I'm not being fair.'

Clarissa sat down on a single chair and told the man to get on with the masks. At four in the morning when he'd finished, she took tape from her bag, wrapped it around the man's arms and legs and across his mouth, and let him sleep on the sofa. She slept in the chair opposite, in what was a fitful night.

Several times, she got a text message from Frank. Each time she'd sent one back saying she wouldn't be long and under no circumstances was he to tell the police that she was missing. She hoped he understood, and when she got out of this, and explained the full story, maybe he'd even forgive her, but for now, she was right where she needed to be.

Chapter 19

Macleod wasn't happy. Yes, he felt at last he may have been getting somewhere based on the three companies that Hope had dragged out of Moore. They had been given to Ross to do some digging and to find out where these companies were potentially meeting in any large numbers. The timescale was in front of them, but where any of these companies were meeting was another question to be answered.

Ross, communicating from home and using his team in the office, had contacted all three of them. On a video call to Macleod and the rest of the team, he explained they were potentially all creating viable targets within the correct time frame.

'Bradley Finance, they are all coming together. It's not a massive company, but it is significant. A meeting of around forty of them within a hotel. Been planned for a few months.'

'And where's that located?' asked Macleod.

'Hotel just on the edge of Inverness, the Highland Hop.'

Macleod had known it. It was a modern hotel used a lot by backpackers and that. It had rooms that could be used for meetings. In some senses, Macleod thought it was a weird selection, but it would have to be covered.

'Cora is also meeting. There's less of them though. Maybe only a half a dozen, but they are the top executives.'

'And, where are they?' asked Susan Cunningham.

'Ah, they're further out, up towards Tain.'

'And what about the last one?' Hope had asked him.

'That's Lynch Accountants. They're on the other side of Inverness. I'm not so sure about this one. It's more like a family fun day. People bringing their partners and kids into work. It's on site, but it has been in the programme for a while. It could be a soft target.'

Macleod had wondered about the three of them, trying his best to pick out which one it would be, but he agreed with Ross. All three were potential targets.

'As there's so many targets,' he had said, 'we'll split up, cover one each. Cunningham, I want you to take Cora, it's smaller. Hope, as you've got the experience, take Lynch Accountants. It's a bit of a different one, lots of open spaces. We need somebody quick on their feet. I'll take Bradley Finance. We'll liaise with firearms, make sure we get teams in position, ready to move, but we do nothing too out front. Can't give away what we know.'

The team had agreed, and in general, Macleod could see more positivity coming from Hope and Cunningham. He backed them up with some experienced uniformed officers, but he was struggling to get more detectives on tap. Certainly not the ones he wanted. It was always the same. He could shift uniform around, he could bring bodies in. He wanted people to be more than bodies. In fairness, several uniforms had stepped up, joined the team in the office, and were carrying out a lot of the work for Ross. Macleod was amazed at the man. Having gone through hell, he could still coordinate, run things, all from a laptop at home. His face seemed to be ever-present on the screen in the office, but his good nature was gone.

Jane was still in a dodgy situation. She had undergone an operation; they told him the next twelve hours would be critical. Then they told him the twelve hours after that would be critical again. Now he stopped asking for them to tell him when was critical until he saw her wake up. He would treat everything as critical.

But he couldn't sit there. He had to be doing. It was killing him. Sitting in a room outside, watching her when she breathed. He'd seen Clarissa, and he wondered if she was on the right track. Did he need to stir things up? He couldn't do it in the way she did it. Not when he was carrying a warrant card. But he was also stretched, so he couldn't charge in anywhere. Hope had only just come back up from Oban. The woman was knackered. So was he.

Everyone was exhausted. To then send someone off chasing, kicking up a fuss. He'd be kicked in the wrong place. Who knew what might happen? No, he'd have to cover off these three, see if they could pick someone else up from there. Then chisel into this horde that was carrying out the killings. They seemed a horde. They had developed into a horde, growing from the small team that dispatched the ministers.

Macleod sat in a van just behind the Highland Hop. It had a burger delivery van written on it. Macleod had a white coat for disappearing out the back. Inside was the communication system to monitor the firearms team and to keep everyone in the loop. CCTV cameras had been set up around the Highland Hop.

Macleod had worked with the firearms team to establish the best route in to take any of the executives of Bradley Finance hostage, or indeed kill them. That seemed the plan now. Go in, build your gallows, hang them, put it on television. The day was raining. It had started with a drizzle. It had then turned into one of those dreich days, clouds hanging in the dark sky.

If we hadn't been closer to summer than winter, the cloud wouldn't have mattered, but this just seems unfair. It lowered his mood, which wasn't good to begin with, but at least he was doing. Albeit, doing was sitting in a burger van watching TV screens.

They got them last time. They caught them coming in. It hadn't worked that badly. In fact, really, they should have done better, but who would have thought someone would explode their own van? This time, firearms officers would stand off more, and a more lethal response had been advised. Stop anyone from pressing any buttons.

With none of his close team here, Macleod felt very much like a spare part. Yes, the firearms officer kept running everything past him, but the attackers would come and this firearms team would decide how to deal with them. Macleod had done his bit. He got the information, albeit non-specific.

The firearms' teams were spread across the three sites, and the budget for everything was running up. The joy of having lunatic killers on the go was loosening of budgets, as the action restraints didn't seem to apply. Well, not at the moment. Not until you caught them and then they'd soon be brought back.

Macleod watched as a van approached. It was black. On the main road, heading round the outskirts of Inverness, it turned off into the Highland Hop. The Highland Hop was on one side of the A9, a new building as you came into Inverness, on what, ex-farming land? Positively tacky, if you believed Macleod.

The road that ran up to it became a car park around it, and you could circumvent it easily in your vehicle. As he saw the black van arrive, there were several other cars in front of it with what looked like tourists. They drove in, seemed to seek the rear of the building, and then parked up before getting out and attending to some luggage in the boot of their car. There was an older man in sunglasses with a hat on. His wife had a headscarf. The kids seem to be of an older age, late teens. Again, they wore dark glasses which confused Macleod.

A second car had a similar family, and they seemed to chat back and forward, but the black van that had come in had stopped at the front. Macleod heard the firearms officer giving the order to approach. As the black van stopped several feet from the front door of the Highland Hop, Macleod watched on the screens. The firearm officers crept forward, maintaining cover, waiting for someone to emerge from the vehicle. No one did. Macleod could hear the officer beside him, tutting.

'That's a weird one,' he said. 'If you pulled up like that, you'd be out on the go. Go find who it is you want. It's not a very subtle arrival.'

'It's not subtle, Macleod. But then, none of the arrivals had been that subtle. If you didn't think anyone was there, you wouldn't . . .'

Macleod sat, eyes fixed on the screen, watching the van. The side door opened on it. Was that a hand easing out? Was there a figure coming with it? Macleod tried to squint on the screen, but he didn't touch any of the controls that made the camera to go in closer.

'What are you seeing, Anderson?' said the man beside him. Anderson barked back, but was told to hold off and await developments. Someone stepped out. They were dressed in a grey monk's habit with the mask. As soon as they did, Macleod could hear the cries of the firearms team.

'Police, halt. On the ground, on the ground,' they said. Macleod watched whoever it was go down to the ground, put his hands behind his back, but there was nobody else following them. He watched as the firearm guys got close, peering in.

'There's no one in the van,' said one of the firearms team.

The door at the rear of the disguised burger van Macleod was sitting in opened, and there were a couple of shots causing Macleod to jump. A few of the men inside clutched at kneecaps and bent over on the floor.

'Don't get up. Don't move. All weapons down.'

Macleod saw a man march in. He had a scarf up across his nose. Thick sunglasses prevented Macleod from seeing the eyes. It might have been a wig he was wearing because Macleod thought he could see a label. The man was carrying a semi-automatic, and he flipped it, driving the butt into the face of the firearms officer beside him. The man crumpled to the floor. 'You,' said the man. 'You.' He was pointing at Macleod.

'No, you don't,' said Macleod. 'No, you don't.' He reached forward and hit a button on the dash in front of him. Alarms went off. They had earpieces in the van. The man who was holding the gun looked at him.

'Idiot,' he shouted, and drove the butt of his gun into the side of Macleod's cheek. Macleod reeled. The pain coursed through him. He rocked and looked like he was going to tip back off his chair, but a couple more hands went underneath his arms and started pulling him out of his seat.

'Get him to the van. Get him to the van.'

Macleod was woozy, but as they pulled him out of the burger van, he was able to catch a glimpse of several people kneeling down and holding rifles, pointing into the distance. The firearms team would come running around that corner.

'Hold back,' shouted Macleod. 'Hold back, they've got you cornered.'

Macleod kicked out at the two men carrying him, but they were strong. He felt the blood trickle from out of his nose from where the rifle butt had slammed into him. Macleod continued to shout, trying to attract attention until the butt of the gun was driven into him again.

As they ran towards the van, he was suddenly thrown down to the ground, and the two men with him bent down, turned, and began shooting towards the corner of the hotel. The firearms team went around the corner, firing back.

'Got you now. You'll pay for this, you bastard.'

Macleod found the words slightly muffled underneath the scarf that was covering the man's mouth, but the eyes that were looking at him were full of hate. The sunglasses had been pulled off, and he hit Macleod again. This time in the gut with the butt of the rifle, before turning back and looking at the picture in front of him.

'We need to go.'

In an exchange of gunfire, before Macleod was hauled up on his feet, a gun was pressed towards his head. 'Anymore and we'll kill him,' came the shout. There was a cry of stand-down issued out to the team around Macleod, and he was dragged over to the van. Once there, his hands were tied up behind him, and he was thrown into it. People had arrived and as a family jumped on board, the door was closed, and the van was driven off.

Macleod knew the police would try to trace it now. There'd be a helicopter up, trying to watch for it, but they'd all missed it. The purpose of this was to get Macleod. He racked his brains. Murray had jumped into the water. Murray had looked to commit suicide. Were they seriously being played all along, or had information got out? Had the plans been changed?

Macleod thought about what had happened. He'd been told to stay off. Jane had been shot. Was this just an extension of that? Had somebody got the word out that Macleod was here at the Highland Hop? There was nothing he could do, though. His face was now against the floor of the van, and someone had a knee in his back.

'We're going to fix you good. You're going to pay for what you did. It's about time you paid.'

Macleod tried to move, but the knee in his back wouldn't allow it, and then he was hit hard in the back of the head. It might have been the gun, but it might have just been a fist. Whatever it was, it was strong enough to knock him out cold.

The next thing Macleod knew, he was sitting, tied in a chair, lights beaming down on his face, caked blood around his mouth, and a dull ache in his head. He looked around the room. It was dark and foreboding, looking like somewhere that had been abandoned a long time ago. Just where was he and what were they going to do with him?

Chapter 20

Hope raced into the Inverness police station car park and jumped out of the car once she had parked it. She made for the steps, ran straight up to the desk sergeant who pointed her to the rear. It was where the operations post was being manned from.

She'd taken the phone call. Macleod had been abducted. Seoras was gone. Seoras was in the hands of those killers. She marched into the room and got a hand held up to her by the woman on the phone. It was Inspector Angela Lambert and she was speaking urgently on the phone. Hope stayed rather frustrated, unable to keep still, and then was brushed by someone marching in with some papers. She realised she was clearly in the way, but she wasn't going anywhere until she found out what was going on.

Angela Lambert put the phone down. 'Early days, we're getting on it with dispatching units. We're trying to trace it.'

'Have you seen it? Have you seen the van?'

'No,' said Lambert. 'The van's gone to ground.'

'Do you need bodies out there? We'll pull the team in. We'll pull them in to go investigate.'

'I need to sit and talk with you about this group. I need to know possible hideouts.'

'We have got nothing on them. The only man I've got is down in Oban. I'll pull his arse back up here,' said Hope. 'See if I can thrash out a base. I'll get Ross to come in. He might have an idea. He's been working on trying to trace these people.'

'Good, but do me a favour,' said Lambert.

'Whatever,' said Hope.

'Get out of my operations room. I need to work. I get you're concerned, but I'll contact you soon as.'

Hope wanted to react. She wanted to tell her about all the times she'd spent with Seoras. He was more than her boss. He was her friend, and they needed to do this and that and everything else in the world to solve this problem. The professional side of her understood. She was in the way. She was emotional, hotheaded, and she was not contributing.

'By the way,' said Lambert, 'the Assistant Chief Constable is at the door. I think Jim wants to talk to you.'

Hope turned around and the look on her face mustn't have been good, for Jim looked at her and gave a wagging finger to show that Hope should follow. She plodded reluctantly out of the room. Jim was at the end of the corridor. Hope walked down it and he stepped into a room at the side. It was a small kitchen area and he closed the door behind her.

'They've got him. They've got Seoras,' said Hope. 'We need to get out there. We need to . . .'

'No, you don't,' said Jim. 'No, you don't.'

'This is Seoras.'

'This is a police officer like any other, and he's been taken by a very hostile group, and we need to be careful what we do and how we do it.'

'They'll kill him.'

'I'm very aware of that,' said Jim, 'but this group has had the runaround on us these last couple of days. I am loath to send officers into places where they could walk into a booby trap. How did you come to pick these areas?'

'What?'

'How did you come about to pick these areas?' asked Jim. 'As I understand it, Seoras told me you were at three different places.'

'Murray, he's down in Oban. I'm getting him brought up now. I need to speak to him again about . . .'

'No,' said Jim. 'He's given you three duff places. Three places that meant your forces are split. They've then gone to one of these places and played a blinder in grabbing Macleod. They put a black van in. Somebody gave themselves up.'

'What does he say?'

'He's dead,' said Jim. 'Somebody believes that Macleod is needed so badly by this group that they're prepared to die. They actually killed themselves.'

Hope stood still, beginning to shake.

'We'll get him,' said Jim. 'We'll get him.'

'Seoras said this was all aimed at him. He said that there was something else going on.'

'What do you mean?' asked Jim.

'When the ministers got taken, they sent cards round everyone from Stornoway, people who had worked there. There was an accusation of abuse there and Seoras being involved. But Seoras wouldn't have been involved. That's not him. The man's incapable of something like that. Incapable of . . .'

'Well,' said Jim, 'Don't tell people what they're capable of and not capable of. Early times, start of his career, who knows?'

'But it's been important to the investigation,' said Hope. 'He

162

wouldn't hide something like that.'

'Where did your information about Stornoway and the people who were there at the time come from? Who interviewed them?'

'Seoras,' said Hope.

'He might be loyal. He might've been covering up something that seemed . . .'

'Don't,' said Hope. Her face was red. Almost as red as her hair. 'This is Seoras Macleod you're talking about. Seoras doesn't mince his words, but he's also as straight as they come. He's by the book. More than that, he makes sure that we go about investigating things in the right way. We could have kicked in a lot of places, in a not-so-nice way and a very un-police worthy way, but he hasn't. Despite the pressure, despite what's going on, because he knows that will come back and they'll get off. He knows it could mean others dying because of the information they're giving out. Don't taint Seoras with some sort of coverup brush.'

'Sit down,' said Jim. Hope looked around her. The little kitchenette didn't really have any decent seats and so she plunked herself up on the sink draining board. The Assistant Chief Commander wasn't the smallest of men, but Hope was six feet tall and sat up even higher. She dwarfed him. He looked up at her.

'I know you work with him. I know he seems too good to be true but we have to temper the person we know with what's coming out. If they believe something happened or it's stored away, there's a good likelihood it did, because of what's going on. We need to get a hold of that story. We need to . . .'

'You need to get him back first. He could be dead soon.'

'Inspector Lambert is doing everything she can to make sure

that's not the case. Trust Lambert; she's good.'

It wasn't that Hope didn't trust Lambert. It was just that Hope needed to be involved in this. She knew the case better.

'Lambert wants to speak to you about the people she's dealing with, and soon. Make yourself available. As for your team, you don't get directly involved in looking for him. You've still got murders to investigate. You've still got to solve this case from your side. The best help you can give Lambert is finding out all the details, including what happened at Stornoway, and why anyone would want to deal with that, whatever it was. Am I understood?'

'Yes, sir,' said Hope. She jumped down off the sink draining board and brushed her way past Jim. As she opened the door to step outside, he called after her.

'Hope, he picked you because he believed you could handle stuff like this. He picked you because he knew you could get above your emotion and deal with things. Prove him right.'

Hope marched out the door, slamming it behind her. She walked to the office, via a flight of stairs, to walk inside and see a team that looked flat.

'Any word on the DCI?' said one of the uniformed officers.

'No, but if there is, I'll be the first to tell you. In the meantime,' said Hope, 'the best thing we can do is understand what's actually going on. See if we can find the people that perpetrated these crimes, so we might shed some light on where they've taken the DCI.'

Hope stormed off into her office, picked up the phone, and called Ross.

'What do you mean, they've got him?'

'They grabbed him,' said Hope. 'They set it up, and they grabbed him.'

'Who would have known Macleod would have been there though?'

'Anyone on the team, people in the station, or maybe they were just going for one of us, any of us.'

'You don't believe that though, do you? They wanted Seoras,' said Ross. 'They wanted Seoras. Do you believe that?'

'Of course, I do,' said Hope.

'How did they know? I'm coming in,' said Ross. 'I'll be there in half an hour. I need to get someone to cover Daniel. Angus is still up in the hospital.'

'We'll see you then. Hurry.'

Hope thought about what she should do next. She would have phoned Jane, except Jane was in the hospital. It was such a mess. *Such a ruddy mess*, she thought. She looked out of the office. No Ross, no Clarissa. *Damn it, Clarissa, I need you now. I need someone to lean on.*

She heard the door opening and saw Cunningham walking into the outer office. Hope walked over to the glass, looking out to the office and banged on it. Everyone looked up and over, but Hope looked back at Cunningham and gave her a finger, showing she should get into the office.

Cunningham opened the door. Hope could see there were almost tears in her eyes.

'How did they just grab him? I mean, how did . . .'

'Enough,' said Hope. 'Enough. I've just had somebody tell me that Macleod trusted me into this position because he knew I could handle it. He trusted you, too. Time to handle things, not for emotion. Get Murray up here from Oban station, see if we can find anything. Ross is coming in as well. We go back over everything we've done, check through, see if there's anything that shows who could do this, or a location.

'We need to give Lambert something to go on. She's going to want to brief me soon about the case, so I'm likely to be out of the picture for an hour. Get Murray up. I'm going to go through that bastard.'

Cunningham gave a nod, and Hope watched her as she turned and marched out. As she opened the door, Hope shouted to her. 'Susan, he'll be okay. You have to trust that. He's going to be good. We've had things before.' Susan nodded, but there was no confidence in the way she did it.

Hope spent the next hour down with Lambert being debriefed on the case so far. There was nothing coming out, nothing to show a place, nothing to indicate where these people were operating from.

'You have got some sort of descriptions on them though,' said Lambert. 'They came in disguised as tourists, family staying over, so there are bits and pieces. We've got a sketch artist working with the firearms team.'

'I believe they went for him,' said Hope. 'I believe they went specifically for Seoras. They needed to know he was there, not in the other two locations we were covering.'

'You're saying there's some sort of mole or something?'

'I don't know. They knew too much.'

Lambert looked angry. 'That's going to make things more interesting,' she said. 'Right, I'll need to keep this much quieter. I don't enjoy doing that with a search. I like everybody able to access all the information and come up with theories.'

When Hope returned up to the office, she had to wait another two hours before Murray arrived at the station. Within five minutes, he was inside the interview suite, Hope sitting in front of him, along with Susan Cunningham.

'Tell me how you knew to set us up?'

166

Murray just laughed.

'Did somebody from in here tell you? Have we got somebody running secrets?'

'Little secrets,' said Murray, 'everywhere. Secrets don't know how to look after themselves, but they knew where he was. Knew it very well.'

Hope leaned forward on the desk. 'Tell me,' she said. 'Tell me and we can make it easier. If not, you'll be an accomplice to kidnapping. If things go bad, an accomplice to murder.'

'Well, it will not be to kidnapping,' said Murray with a wry smile on his face. 'It won't be a . . .'

Hope leapt across the desk. She grabbed the man by the collar, ready to choke the life out of him. Cunningham was up on her feet, pulling at Hope's jacket, taking her back off the man.

'Oh, temper, temper,' said Murray.

'What we need from you,' said Hope, but she found Cunningham still had hold of her. 'Outside please, boss,' she said. Hope turned, walked outside, indignant, looking at Cunningham.

'What are you doing?' said Hope.

'Stopping you from getting done for assault. He will not tell us anything. In the old days, you could have tortured it out of him, put some thumbscrews on him, something like that. Not today. That man will not tell us anything. We're going to need to find out about this some other way.'

Hope went back inside with Cunningham, but sure enough, there were no words to be spoken by the man. Hope returned to her own office and found that Ross had arrived.

'We need to find their location. We need to find out where he's being held. Where do these vans go? Anything. Anything that can link us in.'

'Of course,' said Ross. 'I'm on it, but you've got to understand this is like a needle in a haystack. This won't be easy.'

The telephone rang in Hope's office. She made her way back into it and picked the phone up. It was Frank, Clarissa's husband.

'I realise this might be a bad time,' he said, 'but I can't find Clarissa. She hasn't been back home in over forty-eight hours. I'd phone for a missing person, but it's Clarissa. She is doing things off her own bat. She might be . . .'

The man cried on the other end of the phone.

'I'm sorry,' said Hope. 'I'll try to find her, but no promises.'

Chapter 21

Macleod stared into the bright lights. *There must be six, no, seven,* he thought, trying to count them. They'd been pointed at him for . . . well, he didn't know how long. Since he'd awoken, he heard voices, but the lights were so bright it was hard to see anyone. From time to time, he closed his eyes, and the sweat ran down his face. It was like some crazy cartoon. He was waiting to hear a detective on the other side question him.

Behind him, something was cutting into his wrists. Probably it was plastic cables ties. He could move his arms up and down, but the wrists were tied together. The top half of his body wasn't bound to the chair, but the bottom half was.

Although he was sweating, Macleod also felt the occasional chill across his body. He was wearing only his underpants. They must have stripped him at some point, and his ankles were attached to the chair by use of a cable tie. It was also cutting in around his ankles.

Outside the range of his view, there was shuffling going on. The door opening and closing showed to him that people were coming and going, but no one spoke to him. He heard hushed conversations and a little while ago, he heard, 'Half an hour.'

Half an hour to what, he thought, *or to who*.

The door had clearly been opened again, but unlike previously, this time it stayed open, for the blast of cool air ran across his chest for a longer period. Grey, wispy hairs that covered his chest held huge beads of sweat, adding to the chill.

The lights were suddenly switched off and Macleod found that the room was in a strange grey. His eyes didn't adjust quickly, and he couldn't see into the darkness of it. There was a bit more shuffling and then some lights came on towards the side of the room. He was able to adjust his vision and saw that above him was a rack of nine lights, almost stage lighting, spotlights that would beam down on someone—only they were close, so very close.

The lights now illuminated the room to a degree, and he saw before him thirteen people. He knew this because he could count six on one side, a person in the middle, and a mirror image.

Thirteen, he thought. There really was some number here. They were all wearing grey habits and Macleod felt his heart beat faster. Each wore a mask, but Macleod prepared himself for the speech. They always liked to talk about why they were doing things. They would tell him how they were hard done by and he'd wonder why. He was just a detective trying to solve crime, not a social worker. He would not offer them help. Taking them down, that was his job, but no, they would talk as if justifying what they'd done.

In the middle of the group stood a figure that Macleod thought was a man. When he spoke, the voice was high, but definitely male. He walked forward towards Macleod, stood within touching distance of him, and then turned around to the other twelve who were now seated.

170

'Friends, this is a chance to meet the one who drove me on. This is a chance to go to the start of our crusade. It goes back to a small island, an island just off the west coast of Scotland and it goes back to a small town, to the police station in a small town. For there, the act happened and this man was one of them who turned a blind eye. Tell us about her. Tell us about her, Macleod. Mary Smith. Tell us about Mary Smith.'

Macleod's heart was pounding. Sweat was pouring down his face, for he didn't know what these people would do to him, or rather he suspected he did, but Mary Smith? He hadn't known a Mary Smith. He thought back. Mairi Smith—he remembered a Mairi Smith.

'Do you mean Mairi? That's how they spell it in the Gaelic. Mairi Smith, she was my mother's friend. She was . . .'

The man spun round and with the back of his hand, struck Macleod right on the cheek. The blow had come from some distance away and Macleod felt his head snap to the left, his face stinging.

'Don't mock me. Mary Smith, tell us about Mary Smith.'

'I do not know a Mary Smith,' said Macleod. 'I do not know what you are talking about. Enlighten me.'

The man turned around, knelt down in front of Macleod, his mask now close to Macleod's face. 'Will you not tell them? Will you not admit your guilt?'

'I do not need to admit of guilt, and if I do, it'll be to my God, not to someone I haven't wronged. You need to admit to your guilt, you hung people. You . . .'

Macleod nearly threw up as a punch was delivered straight into his stomach.

'We're not here to talk about us. We're not the guilty ones. You are the guilty one of many guilty ones. You'll tell us about it.'

Macleod breathed heavily. His eyes were on the point of tears, but he fought them back. Years ago, he could have taken a beating. He could have taken the punches like they were nothing. He could have steeled himself to someone like this, spat in his face, but now age was catching up. Every blow hurt these days, every one.

'Speak, Macleod, speak. Tell us your sin.'

Your sin? thought Macleod. *Not what you did, not your mistake or your evil, but your sin?* It reminded him of growing up at home, being asked to confess your sin by the man in black at the front with the white collar. He had no right to speak to him like that. No right to act like he was some sort of minister. These were the people that had killed them.

'Speak, Macleod,' said the man, again. 'Speak, or we'll make you.'

'I don't know the woman you speak of. I don't know any Mary Smith. Would you listen to me? I do not know what you're talking about.'

The man stood up in front of Macleod, turned his back, and from Macleod's position seemed to cross his arms in front of his chest. The members of the group stood up and slowly they filed round so that they now all stood in front of Macleod. A man walked up and unloaded a punch to Macleod's face that sent the chair toppling backwards. Macleod's jaw felt like it was broken and his arms were trapped underneath his own weight as he fell, unable to get them clear of the chair crashing onto the floor. He yelled out in pain.

But the chair was whipped up and someone else was there. It looked like a woman. She slashed him, scrabbing him across his chest so that he bled. Was it her nails? Was it the teeth of some knuckle duster? He didn't know, but the pain was real. One after another they beat him, until by the time the last had been, he was a hanging wreck on the chair. Staring down at his own feet, he heard the whispered words again. 'Tell us, Macleod. Tell us about Mary Smith.'

'I don't know Mary Smith,' said Macleod. 'I have never known a Mary Smith. If you mean the Gaelic, my mother's friend Mairi Smith was . . .'

He felt another punch to the face. This time a tooth came loose. He half spat it out, watching it fall limply on the ground in front of him.

'I see our inspector's still unable to recall things. We shall encourage him again.'

Macleod was bounced this way and that. The chair fell over four times, once because he was kicked in the head. By the time they placed him back up in the chair, it was all he could do to open his eyes and try to look at them. There was blood over his body. He could tell he was heavily bruised. His jaw felt wrong. His tooth had come out. The nose was possibly broken and there was a cut above his eye that was leaking blood down the side of his face.

'Tell us, Macleod, tell us about Mary Smith.'

'I know nothing of Mary Smith,' he said in defiance, and then choked on the blood at the back of his throat. 'You have the wrong man. If you'll tell me what it is, I'll investigate it. I'll find out what happened.'

'We should present some evidence to the inspector, shouldn't we?'

Macleod had various letters held in front of him. He couldn't make out most of the words, but he saw at the bottom of each piece of paper a name. One was McNeil, one was Henderson.

There was a clerk, Anna Beeton. He desperately tried to scan the words above the names, but he couldn't read them. His eye kept half closing. His brain was in fog and the last piece of paper said Macleod.

'It's written there. Seoras Macleod. It's written there. It says Macleod, the letter written to you. Written to you, asking you to protect them, asking you to deal with it. She was not ready. She was far off being ready, that he sated himself on her. Yet he took her away. Took away and ruined what was left of her childhood.

'She's never got over it. She never got over it until she went to the place where we all have peace. That's the only peace there is from evil like that. I don't blame you for not being able to give her peace, but you could have given her justice. You could have looked harder. Could have not turned a blind eye. Could have not covered it up.'

'I don't know,' said Macleod, eyes streaming with tears, and the pain so unbearable. 'I don't know of who you speak. I don't know of what you speak.'

'Liar,' said the man, and suddenly all the surrounding voices were shouting. 'Liar, liar.' They called him names in the coarsest of tones. Names he wouldn't have spoken. Words he would never have used. Foul language. And then they spoke about what they'd do to him, how they would correct this wrong that he'd been involved in.

'It's time to pay your debts, Macleod. It's time to own up.'

Macleod couldn't lift his head. The room was spinning. His head was swooning, and he felt like he was going to collapse. Felt like the world was ending. They paraded around, each delivering a blow, but this time some of them were using implements, some that cut into you, some that were just heavy

174

and battered you. He felt a knife being pressed against his neck, an incision made, and blood coming out, but then taken away before anything irreversible had happened.

'I'm not as good as this as you are, am I?' said the man who was leading them all. 'We will dispose of you, whatever you don't say, and I will do it to our public. I will put it up for people to watch. The great Macleod, Oh, man of justice.'

Macleod felt the man spit in his face. 'But you weren't born in justice. You were born in a coverup. You were born looking after your own.'

'What are you talking about?' screamed Macleod. 'In the name of all that is good and holy, what are you talking about?'

'Don't fool me, don't mess with me, don't piss me about, Macleod. I'll gut you and watch them sitting on the floor. It's time for your sins to be examined, for you to be weighed and you to be judged. How do we find him?'

'Guilty,' said a voice on the left. 'Guilty,' said a high-pitched one. One after another, 'Guilty,' was said. Macleod's head was spinning. The nightmare was rolling on and on. He did not know what they were talking about, nothing. He tried to rack his mind, back to Stornoway, back to growing up, back to being a police officer. It was when he was a police officer; they were talking about justice, but McNeil? McNeil was a good man. All those people, they were good people. They didn't cover stuff up. He was a religious sod, at worst, McNeil.

'I think it only fitting that, as someone who says they're devoted to the man of sorrows, that you go out like him. Whip him,' said the man, 'but make sure he stays alive. I want to be there. I want to watch him suffer.'

Macleod couldn't raise himself on the seat. Instead, he hung from his arms, a plastic cable tie holding the wrists together, forming a bond around the back of the chair that was not going away. It left Macleod hanging forward. He heard the crack and felt the pain at the same time they whipped him. The whip came in from the side, and from over the top. Something on the end of it cut into him. He felt about three blows, and then he blacked out.

Chapter 22

Clarissa was not in a good mood. The rain was coming down, and while she could be the outdoors type when she wanted to be, she liked to be striding around seeing nature. Woodland walks, maybe fishing, grouse shooting. She'd done that as well. But this was not the highlights of nature. This was sitting in a bush on a council estate with the rain falling.

She couldn't move far either, for the bush wasn't that big. She had a cape on instead of the usual shawl, this one waterproof, and a hat on her head. But the rain was annoying. It was that constant rain, that steady drizzle that bore into you slowly. There were also midges, or 'The height of evil,' as Clarissa called them.

She had, fortunately, been able to spray her face with the repellent, but she'd found out that the repellent only stopped them from biting. They still landed, they still hovered around you. They still formed almost a black beard around your chin. With the wind so still, and being inside the bush as well, Clarissa thought she must be the perfect landing ground for them.

It had been three hours since the drop had been made. New

masks now lying in a bag at the bottom of a bin. Apparently, the bin wouldn't be emptied for another three days, but it was still half full. The masks, however, were not sitting on top. The creator had placed them carefully in a bag and had placed that bag at the bottom of the bin. He'd had to hoke for a bit, but he had done it quickly. Having done it, Clarissa had escorted him to an empty house of a couple she knew and tied him up to a chair just in case he was playing games.

Right now, she thought the possibility he was playing games was high, but then she saw the man at the end of the street. He was young, maybe twenty-three, twenty-four, and walked with an air of someone that didn't care about anything. He was on his way to somewhere, except he wasn't. For as he passed the bin, he stopped. He looked left; he looked right, and checked his surroundings. Then he turned and took the top of the bin off.

These days, the bins comprised a metal interior with a plastic exterior that slid over the top. That plastic exterior now removed, the man delved down and sure enough brought up the package that had been dropped there three hours earlier. The man placed the bag inside a black rucksack that he was carrying and zipped it up. He glanced around again before putting the plastic exterior of the bin back on. He turned then and started walking down the street quietly, but with obvious intent. Clarissa stayed put, watching him disappear until he got to the corner, at which point she emerged from her bush.

Her hand swept along her cape and down her trews, moving away every trace of twig or excess leaf that had fallen on her. She began to walk down the street, feeling the pain of her previous injuries, but her mind was set. She took out her phone, placed a call, and waited for the other end to pick up.

'Dear McGrath,

'You might want to know that a new delivery of masks has just been picked up from the Inverness area. They're on the move, hopefully, to where these crazy people have a base. I'm on the trail and will keep you informed.'

'New number?' said Hope. 'What's the deal, Clarissa?'

'Let's just say I'm off-grid. That's how they put it these days, isn't it? That's the modern expression.'

'I need to know everything,' said Hope. 'Clarissa, they've taken Seoras.'

'What?' she replied, her heart beginning to beat faster.

'I said they've taken Seoras. They grabbed him. It's not widely known outside the force.'

Clarissa could feel her pace quickening. She rounded the corner and saw her mark further up the street. 'When I find out where he's going, I'll let you know.'

'Be careful,' said Hope. 'These are killers.'

'Understood.'

Clarissa closed down the call. Hope would have her number now. She may even trace it, but for now, he was on the move. She believed that Hope would have the good sense not to interfere in her tail.

They got Seoras. Again, Clarissa's heart beat again quicker. She could feel a degree of sweat under her hat, but she didn't know if that was the rather muggy feel of the day. Maybe she was having to exercise harder than she had done for a long time.

She had got herself into this because of the attacks on Angus and Jane, Macleod's partner. But now they'd gone for him? She could feel the anger building up inside. She'd tear them apart for this if they'd laid a finger on him. And yet another part of her could feel that cold seeping in, the cold that said he's already dead. They've got him, they've killed him, and they'd have hung him or butchered him in some gruesome fashion.

She'd seen what they'd done to the ministers. She'd heard what they'd done to the chief executives of that company. But why Macleod? Why had they gone for Seoras? The initial warning off was expected, but to come after a police inspector, a chief inspector at that, doing his job? They must have realised the force would be after them. The force would react to this. They wouldn't be safe wherever they went.

Clarissa tried to keep her mind on the job. She was tailing. She needed to stay focused. They had walked a good twenty minutes now into the centre of Inverness. Clarissa followed them through the bus station, then through a small car park and into the rear of the train station.

She kept a distance as she saw them looking up at the departures board, trying to estimate where they were going. It was an Edinburgh train they were looking at. It would head off, Carrbridge, Aviemore, then further south. *They couldn't be going that far though*, thought Clarissa. Most of their operation lately had been close to Inverness. Maybe it was harder to run with a larger number of people.

She watched the man buy a ticket in an automated machine and cursed her luck. She looked up at the next three trains leaving and bought herself a ticket on each of them. For a moment, she wondered if she'd get these back on expenses, considering the fact she was working rogue. But then the wildfire settled in again, but it was time to watch. It was time to keep an eye on this man.

They opened up the gates at the front, allowing passengers to place their tickets in the automatic machine. Then he headed for Platform 3, where the train to Edinburgh waited. It was four coaches, typically ScotRail in fashion. Clarissa followed the man, noting that he'd got on at the first door. She walked past, glancing in at the train and saw him move down it. He'd gone through one carriage into the second before he took up a seat. Clarissa made her way to the end of that carriage before entering and then located herself approximately six seats away, sitting on the aisle end.

The train departed, the rain still falling outside, and Clarissa pretended to look out the window. Although, for the first part of the journey, there were trees by the sidings yard of the train station. They were out into the countryside surrounding Inverness. Green and lush, with the odd viaduct, she saw a bridge and immense sweeping landscapes.

The day was grey, however, which meant that the picture didn't have its usual sheen and sunshine. This part of the world was stunning. When it was raining, it was merely very good. A man caught Clarissa on the shoulder as he tried to push past her seat and she stared up at him. He glanced back, and she noted he left the carriage before returning. He walked up and down three times, each time he was looking at her, staring intently when he walked past again. She noted he nodded at the man and the bag. She stood up, and instead of following the second man, she just turned around and went down to the toilet area in between her carriage and the third carriage.

As she left the second carriage, she took a quick glance backwards and saw that the man was following her. She stepped to one side, pressed the door button on the toilet, and heard the large door sweep away. It was one of those half-rounded cubicles, set up so that people with wheelchairs could get in easily, as well as those who walked.

The door was closing again as the man entered this third carriage. He was staring at the toilet, raced forward, put his hand in the door, stopping it before it closed. He was primed, ready to jump through that door as it now opened again. When it had got just big enough so that he could step through, Clarissa grabbed him from behind, driving him into the cubicle and smacking his head off the far wall.

She hit the close-door button with one hand, still holding the dazed man with the other. As the door slid back, she smacked his head again off the wall and he tumbled to the floor. She kicked him hard in the stomach, and again, and a third time, before dropping to her knees and turning him over. He was groaning, but she took some handcuffs, slipped them on his wrists before pulling out a large handkerchief and tying it around his mouth. When it looked like he was about to stir, she caught him with her boot across the jaw, knocking him out.

'You just sit there.'

She pressed the door open and closed it again before looking up and down for a conductor. It took her a couple of minutes to find him, but when he came along, she put on a rather teary face and sniffed at him.

'You need to close that off. It's flowing everywhere. I mean, there's just, it's horrible, the excrement, excrement,' she said in her posher voice.

'What's happened?' asked the conductor.

'It's come back up through the toilet. There's poo everywhere. Oh, excrement, it's disgusting.'

The man went to open the door. She put his hand on his quickly, grabbing it and turning him towards her.

182

'Don't, don't go in there. It's not safe. You'll need to get a proper cleaning crew. Lock it off. Lock off the door. Seal it out of order and no one can go in. Probably best you wait until Edinburgh to clean it. You might need to take the carriage out of service.'

The man looked at her. 'Is it that bad?'

Clarissa looked down at her shoes. 'If I had any others, I'd change them.' The man stepped back slightly and then turned and took out a key, placing it into a slot. The door came up as locked with a brief message on it saying, 'Out of order.'

'Well, I'm very sorry for your inconvenience. There's another toilet further down if you wish to use that. If you wish, I'll take your shoes and clean them for you.'

'That would be excellent,' said Clarissa. She slipped them off, giving them to the man and explained to him she'd sit in the third carriage. She found a seat and got some strange looks from people, but her boots were returned five minutes later. The man had obviously sprayed something on them because they were fragrant. 'Again, my apologies, ma'am,' he said. 'We'll get that sorted.'

'Not at all. You've been magnificent,' she said. 'Hasn't he?' She turned to the man sitting opposite her, who looked rather bemused and a little stunned. 'I said, hasn't he been terrific?'

'Oh, absolutely,' said the man, not understanding what she was on about. Clarissa stood up and marched back towards the second carriage, but could feel the train coming to a halt. She looked outside at the signs slowly stopping and saw the word Aviemore. A quick glance down the carriage and she saw the rucksack disappearing out one door. She stepped out and picked up her mobile phone.

'Hope, I'm in Aviemore. He's got off the train here. I don't know where he's going. I'll try to call you when I can. Oh, and I left his keeper disabled in the toilets on the train. Don't worry, it's out of order, but you could do with sending someone to it.'

'Wait, Clarissa. I need to . . .'

Clarissa hung up. The man was disappearing out of Aviemore station, and Clarissa followed. *Where would he go from here? Were they based in Aviemore itself? Because if they weren't, you were looking at the Cairngorm Mountains.*

He could get a bus, he could get a taxi, he could get picked up by someone else, which would be a pain. This wasn't London, where you wave your arm and grab a cab. It could be a problem to keep a tail on him.

The rain had not gone away, and it was still pouring as she left the cover of the Aviemore train station. The man turned right, heading up towards the town, and Clarissa wondered exactly where he was going. *I'm coming, Seoras*, she thought, *I'm coming for you.*

Chapter 23

Hope stepped out into the rain in Aviemore and looked up and down it. It had been forty-five minutes since Clarissa had called. Susan Cunningham was standing beside her, looking up and down the street as well.

'Well, I can't see her. I know you know her better than me, but she doesn't seem to be about.'

'I wonder where he's gone,' said Hope.

'But where do we go?' said Susan. 'I mean.'

'We're as close to her as we can be,' said Hope. 'We have to wait for her, we have to.'

'You could call her.'

'I could,' said Hope. 'And I just have. There's no answer. In fact, there's no ringing on the phone. It's gone straight to an answering machine. She's closed the phone down or she's out of signal. I doubt she would've closed the phone down. She'd have wanted us to trace her.'

'And on that front,' said Susan.

'On that front, Ross is doing it. He's also checked where she was. The call she made was from a residential estate and he believes she made her way through to the train station and down to here. That's confirmed by what she said on the phone. Where she's gone from here, however, who knows?'

'Do you want me to ask people? I mean, if it's Clarissa, she sticks out. She's got that look about her.'

'No,' said Hope. 'The last thing we need to do is to attract attention to her.'

'But this is Seoras. If she is walking into anything, if they get her before she has time to contact us . . .'

Hope knew that there was something in what Susan Cunningham was saying. You were looking at an older woman, well, at least for a police officer, but Hope knew Clarissa could look after herself. She was anything but daft.

The only thing that Hope prayed was that the red mist wouldn't come down. Hope could feel herself shaking inside. *How long since they'd taken Seoras? So far, they had shown nothing on TV, broadcasted it, or made a call. They'd said nothing, nothing about him. He must still be alive. That's what you've got to keep telling yourself. That's what you've got to keep saying.*

'What do we do?' asked Susan.

'We wait. Seoras once said to me I had to trust the team. Stop trying to do everything myself and at the moment, I want to do everything. I want to get him back more than you'll ever know, Susan. He would tell me, 'Trust the team.' We need to trust Clarissa.'

'But she's not even part of the team,' said Susan. 'She left, she . . .'

'Enough,' said Hope, firmly, but quietly. 'She's always been part of the team. Seoras knew she was going off half-cocked and he let her go. He doesn't do that because he can't be bothered to stop her. Seoras did that because he thinks it's going to get us places. He thinks it's going to break an investigation open that, frankly, we've gone nowhere with. He's not a man that does that lightly. I just hope it's going to save his life.'

* * *

Sometime earlier, Clarissa had seen her man step inside a car and drive away. Clarissa scanned quickly for taxis and had seen none, but there was a man sitting, a young man, in a rather smart car. She wasn't sure what he was doing, whether he was waiting for someone or he'd just parked up to enjoy his drink, or whether indeed, he was about to do something. Clarissa opened the passenger door that was nearest to the curb and got in.

'What the hell do you think you're doing?' cried the man.

'Shut up,' said Clarissa. 'Shut up and drive.'

'Do what? What do you mean, shut up and drive?'

'I said, shut up and drive or someone's going to die.'

The man looked frightened. He went to turn for his door but Clarissa grabbed his arm.

'Don't, that's unwise. I'm telling you that someone's going to die if you don't shut up and drive.' The man put his hands on the wheel. 'Slowly,' said Clarissa. 'Make sure you don't cause anyone else to panic. We're just driving nicely. Off we go.'

The man's hands were shaking on the wheel, but the car drove out smoothly enough into the lane of traffic. Clarissa looked up ahead. The car her quarry had got into was red, an old Ford, and was heading straight out of town.

'Straight ahead,' said Clarissa, calmly. 'And just remember—'

'I know,' said the man. 'There's no need to threaten me.'

'I'm not threatening,' said Clarissa.

'Of course not,' said the man. His eyes were glued on the road, but every now and again, he would turn and look at her.

'You don't look the type,' he blurted.

'Oh, there are many types,' said Clarissa. 'Turn right in three junctions' time.'

She'd watched the Ford turn right, and when they turned right as well, she could see it was not far up ahead. The road was heading out into the hills, which is exactly what she didn't want. If they were going somewhere with no one around, it was going to be difficult to attempt any sort of rescue. She may have to wait until backup arrived. Until she knew where they were going, there was no point. No doubt Ross was tracing her phone, anyway.

'Where am I going?' said the man.

'I'm not sure yet,' said Clarissa, 'But I'll tell you when you can stop. Thank you for your assistance.'

'I wouldn't call it assistance.'

'I would,' said Clarissa. 'If you didn't assist me, someone was going to die, so that to me sounds like assistance.'

The man looked down. Clarissa kept one hand deliberately underneath her shawl.

'What have you got under your shawl?' asked the man suddenly. 'Is there a knife?'

'That's rude,' said Clarissa. 'At my age, you're asking me what I have under my shawl. What do you think this is? Just keep your eyes on the road. Do as you're told.'

The man looked bemused, but he was still nervous enough to obey. Clarissa hoped he stayed that way.

'Were you waiting for someone in town?' she asked.

'I was, actually. My girlfriend. She's going to be pissed when she gets back and there's no car there.'

'What's she like?' asked Clarissa.

The man eyed her suspiciously. 'She's nice.'

'No,' said Clarissa. 'I asked you what she was like. Let's see. She'd be blonde, won't she? You look like a man that likes blondes.'

'Yes, she is. How did you know that?'

Good guess, thought Clarissa. 'Long legs,' said Clarissa. 'You are a man that likes long legs. More of an elegant girl, not like me.' The man looked at her strangely. 'I meant when I was younger. Hello. There's something to be said for an older woman. Next left.'

The man looked back at the road quickly and took a left. They were a little back from the red Ford and there were two cars in between them, which was keeping Clarissa happy for the moment.

'Well, I mean, she's not a buxom lass, is she?' The man looked at her again. *When did the word buxom not become part of the English language? Young people nowadays, they don't know words. They don't know what people are saying.*

'She's more of a beanpole than a pear?' Clarissa was struggling now.

'She wouldn't like you calling her a beanpole.'

'No, but I'm right, aren't I? Long blonde hair, long legs, looks like a beanpole. Nice white teeth, though.' She could see the man beginning to shake.

'Have you got her somewhere?'

'I haven't got her anywhere,' said Clarissa. 'I haven't even met her.'

'Oh, that's it,' said the man. 'You've got somebody else to get her.'

'All I'm saying is that if you don't drive, somebody will die,' said Clarissa.

'Whatever then,' said the man. 'Whatever, okay? Just don't do anything rash. Don't get them to do anything daft.'

'I'm hoping nobody does anything daft because if they do, somebody might die.' Clarissa was playing with her words, but inside she knew each one of them was true.'

The Ford ahead took a left and when Clarissa followed, she was the only car on the road with him. She saw it turn off, heading down a track rather than a proper road. As her impromptu taxi went past the track, Clarissa told her driver to pull in.

The rain was still coming down, and there was a certain mistiness around the area. Clarissa thought this was a good thing. She turned to the man in the car.

'You're going to wait here for ten minutes. After that, you're going to drive into Aviemore. You're going to find the nearest police station. You're going to say to them that DI Hope McGrath needs to know that the older woman is now out of town, and you're going to tell them exactly where this is.'

Clarissa picked up her phone and told the man to write down some coordinates from her GPS. She noted there was a signal, but barely.

'We're quite high up here,' she said, 'ten minutes back, find a police station. Don't dilly-dally. If you do all that for me, I'm sure you'll find your girlfriend waiting for you in town. She might not be in the best mood, but she'll be unharmed.'

'Whatever,' said the man. 'Whatever I need to do, just don't harm her.'

'I won't harm her,' said Clarissa. 'No intentions of it.'

Clarissa walked off in the rain towards the track that the car had taken. She didn't step onto the track, but went out into the small, wooded area beside it and walked alongside it. Keeping about twenty yards off it, she climbed up over a hill where she could see a large house. It was set back off the road. There were trees around it, and it certainly would be hard to see. There were other outbuildings around it.

Clarissa stayed down low in what cover there was. She had green tartan trews on. The outer cover of the shawl was green. Everything was in her favour except for her hair, so she pulled her hat down tight.

She picked up her phone and saw she had a small signal, but decided against calling, and put the phone back inside her shawl again. It took Clarissa a good twenty minutes to get up to the house, and from the outside, it looked bleak. It was big, but it was rather run down. A lot of the paint beginning to flake, but she saw an outhouse, a rather large barn, and she saw people occasionally walking back and forward.

They didn't look like the people who would live here, but then again, who would live in a house like this? Somebody who liked the quiet, somebody who had been here for a long time. Or maybe someone who didn't have the money to afford to do the place up but didn't want to live in that metropolis they call Aviemore. She chuckled to herself.

She knew she was just trying to keep her mind from thinking about what she would find. Macleod was out there somewhere, possibly in here. She'd need to find him. Clarissa stayed in the undergrowth, staying low, and could see the occasional person outside. They were searching, scanning the area with their eyes.

That was the thing about having somewhere like this. Did they have CCTV outside? She struggled to find any cameras. If you didn't have cameras, you couldn't see. You'd have to send someone out, but if you had cameras, people would wonder why such a ramshackle place would have them.

The group was lying in cover, but they were lying wide out in the open. It was the best cover, to be there but not seen, to be in someone's face but not be who they thought you were.

Clarissa moved across to the outhouse. As she did so, a large barn door swung open. Two men in grey habits appeared with masks on. They had an arm under some poor hopeless soul, each carrying him from either side. The man's feet dragged along the ground, and he was only wearing a pair of underpants. There was blood around him. It looked like they'd smashed him to a pulp. He was breathing though, even an occasional moan.

She was some distance away, and it was hard to see, but Clarissa stole up. Reaching a tree at the edge of the driveway of the building, she got to a point where she was maybe forty yards away. She had to put her hand to her mouth to stop a gasp coming out, as the head of the man swung unintentionally towards her. It was Seoras. They'd done that to Seoras.

Clarissa's blood was boiling, but she wasn't stupid. She waited until they'd taken Macleod inside, and she stepped away some fifty yards into a copse of trees. She looked down at her phone. There was a signal, barely. She called Hope.

'What is it?' asked Hope. 'Where are you?'

'Where I am right now is where Seoras is. I've just seen him, Hope. They've battered him. They've bloody battered him. I think they're going to kill him. They're . . . Dear God, Hope, they have . . .'

'Calm down,' said Hope. 'Where are you? Tell me where you are.'

Clarissa looked down at her phone. She pressed the app for

the GPS, and she read out the coordinates.

'Stay there. It won't be long till we can get there. Stay there. We're coming with a full team. We'll get him,' said Hope. 'Just do nothing rash.'

'They've taken him inside. They're going to . . . I think they're going to kill him. I think they're going to . . .'

'Stay put. We're on our way. Do you hear me? Do you hear me? Clarissa, do you hear me?'

But the call had gone dead.

Chapter 24

'I can't wait,' Clarissa said to herself. 'I can't wait. Hope is wrong. I need to see him. I need to make sure he is all right.'

She stole up again through the grass and the trees and reached the driveway of the house. Everyone seemed to move inside and soon the driveway was deserted, but they were all heading to the building that they dragged Macleod into. Clarissa didn't like the look of this.

She wasn't great at cover or understanding the best way to approach a building with people inside. In the past she'd had to, but not with so much at stake. What could she do? Her mind was abuzz and her stomach was nearly sick having seen Macleod, but inside was a determination that had served Clarissa well for most of her career.

'Macleod's Rottweiler,' she said to herself. 'They call me Macleod's Rottweiler. Time to bare the teeth,' she said.

Time to do what? It was all right, building herself up, but she knew she was no one-man army. Or one-woman army, for that matter. She could handle herself in a fight. Yes, to a point, but she was no Jackie Chan. She didn't march into a room and take out everybody else. She'd need to find out where he was, first, at least then if Hope turned up, she'd be able to point.

She stole across the driveway, wincing at the sound the stones made under her feet. But the rain was coming down so hard that she thought it might drown out any movement she made. *God bless the rain*, she thought. It was banging up against the windows now and the wind was picking up.

She'd read once that in Japan, back in the days of the ninjas, these assassins loved the wet nights with the wind and the rain, for it masked their approach. She doubted any of them had approached in a waterproof reversible tartan shawl and trews. Neither did she think any of them had approached with more determination to achieve their goal.

Clarissa leaned up against the wall of the house, sliding along to a window and peeking in. She could see a large room, and in the middle of that room was Macleod. They'd plonked him on the floor. His hands were now tied behind him. She was unsure of what they were going to do other than kill him, for she saw a body bag being brought into the room.

Clarissa had made a count, and there were over twenty people in that room. Outside of pitching in with a submachine gun and spraying the room with bullets, she couldn't see how she was going to extract Macleod. If there had only been two or three, she could have given it a go. Even then, she'd have lost the element of surprise after the first one.

There needed to be a panic. There needed to be . . . Clarissa moved away from the window, back to the wall. Surely, there had to be something else around here. Something else that would cause a distraction. Preferably, it would go boom, or be something that sent out a blinding light. But what would do that?

Clarissa quickly made her way to the outbuilding. The door

was shut, but she pulled it back and stepped inside. There was a corridor with several rooms off it, but she could hear no one. Had they all gone up to the big room? Were they all there to witness Macleod dying?

She'd raced down the corridor. It was plain white, with dirty marks across it, but she noticed one room had blood on the handle. She peered inside.

In the middle of the floor, there was copious amounts of blood, as if someone had bled onto it. Was that where they'd had Seoras? She saw whips, she saw cudgels, and then she said, 'Stop it. Focus, Clarissa, focus on what you have to do.'

She ran down to the next room. There was nothing. The room after that, however, was a store. There were methylated spirits and other painting items. Spirits to clean your brushes, but spirits were light. She looked around and saw a stick and several blocks of wood. There were rags in the far corner. She could make a brand out of these items. She could certainly get a fire going.

Quickly, she grabbed one of the larger sticks, wrapped some rags around it, and poured methylated spirits over it. But there were no matches because why would you keep matches along with methylated spirits? You'd be asking for trouble. She needed to find something to light it.

Clarissa searched the room, but there was nothing. She went back out and searched each room along the corridor. There was nothing to light the damn thing with. She exited the building still carrying the stick with the methylated spirits rag on the end.

She'd have to go inside the main house, and she didn't have time to mess about. Quickly, she ran around the back of the house, hoping that everyone was stuck in that room in the front. The back door was open. She wandered around the kitchen.

The room was warm, unlike the outbuilding, and she realised there were old-style radiators here. There must have been a boiler somewhere. She looked around the kitchen, opening cupboards as quietly as she could. Where were the matches? There must be some matches.

She found a blowtorch, the small catering variety. What the hell was that doing here? Finishing the top of meringues while they killed people? She looked through a small drawer that held knives and forks and other accoutrements, and she saw one of those clickers for igniting a gas cooker.

She looked around and saw it, the gas cooker. There must be bottles outside. She turned on the gas, opening it up fully, but not using the clicker. She closed the back door, took the clicker with her as well as the blowtorch, and then shut all the kitchen doors behind her.

'Think,' she said to herself. 'Think, how do I do this?'

From inside the front room, she heard people talking, and she snuck up to the door. It was old style, had a lock with a keyhole. She was able to bend down and look through that keyhole. From what she could make out, Macleod was now hung up.

His hands above him. In front of him stood a man in a mask. They were all in masks now. All in grey monks' habits and masks. Clarissa stepped away from the door. She took the blowtorch and, using the clicker, lit it. With it, she lit the rag around her stick and watched the fire burn on it. She went over to the wallpaper, held it close, and the wallpaper started to take.

Clarissa didn't know how many layers of wallpaper were

197

underneath, but this house was old. This was no fireproof, modern building designed to extinguish and control any fire that happened. This was old school. It would burn. She watched as the fire spread along the wall. From inside, she could hear voices.

'Tell us about her. Tell us about Mary Smith. How did you cover it up? Tell us what you did to her.'

'Don't know. Don't know Mary Smith.'

Macleod's voice was weak, but he was fighting with everything he could to tell them. From her viewpoint, she could see his toes were barely touching the ground while his hands were held up above him. The man stepped forward, hitting Macleod again in the stomach, over and over until he made him vomit.

'We've asked you to admit your crime, but no more. We'll slice you open like they used to do. You can watch your entrails as you die. Appropriate for a man with no guts. A man not able to stand up for others.'

Clarissa looked around her. *Where the hell was Hope? Why wasn't she here yet?* There was no time. She grabbed the brand that she'd made for herself, that was still burning, and with the other hand, she took the door handle. It turned and Clarissa threw open the door.

'You don't lay a finger on him. Get the hell away.'

Clarissa ran forward and hit one of the monk's robes with the brand. It lit up immediately, and the man started screaming.

'Get her,' shouted the man who had been in front of Macleod. Several turned, and Clarissa swung the brand back and forward. She didn't know what to do. How was she going to face all of them? How was she going to . . .

An almighty explosion rocked the building. The wall behind

them blew out into the room, knocking everyone off their feet except for Macleod. He was swinging from his bonds.

As Clarissa tried to recover a sense of what was going on, she realised that the gas in the kitchen had exploded. Windows at the front of the room had blown out, and a fire was raging. Several of the monk's habits had caught fire, and they were screaming and running here and there.

Clarissa ran for Macleod, desperate to get him down. She flung her arms around him, trying to pull him, but all he did was cry out in pain. She turned to where she'd dropped her own brand. It was still alight. She ran for it, picked it up as one monk approached her. She swung at him, but he turned and fled. His mask had been knocked to one side, and part of him was bleeding heavily.

Clarissa ignored him, ran back to Macleod, and lifted the brand up above him. She watched as the flames took the rope and it burned. He was still hanging thirty seconds later until the last of the strands had caught fire. He dropped like a sack of potatoes to the floor, his feet unable to support him.

Clarissa reached down, put Macleod's arm around her neck, and tried to pick him up. She could barely do it and half dragged him away from a room that was becoming an inferno. The path to the hallway was blocked off. Too many of the monks were running around. She took the door on the other side of the room. Only when she got through, did she realise it led to a single room, a little annex off the larger room.

She went to turn with Macleod to leave, but someone pushed her and, together with Macleod, she clattered into the wall behind them. Clarissa's head smacked off it and she felt distinctly woozy, but when her eyes looked up, there was no mistaking the man in the gown. That grey, evil mask looking at her, motionless. The other thing that caught her eye was the machete in the man's hand.

'I'd said I'd gut him in there. He can watch his own entrails. You can watch yours as well.'

'He's innocent,' said Clarissa. 'Listen here, he's innocent.'

'Oh, no!' cried to man. 'He let them do it to Mary Smith. He didn't come after them. A policeman! He's meant to protect people. He's meant to ensure justice. Well, this time the justice comes to him.'

The man raised the machete, about to throw it down onto Macleod's head, when Clarissa reached up, grabbing the man's wrist. He kept pushing, and she could barely hold his hand up. The man took her hand off his wrist, reached down, and grabbed Clarissa by the throat. He squeezed hard, and she struggled. Her hand desperately reached for his.

'An old bloody woman. An old bloody bitch comes to save you. Not this time, Macleod. Not this time. You're going to pay.'

Clarissa was pushed, driven back into the wall, where her head again connected. She almost blacked out, but her eyes opened to the horror of the man lifting the machete again with two hands and about to come down on top of Macleod. As he went to swing, Clarissa saw someone come through the door.

They jumped at the man, grabbing both his wrists, stopping the blade from descending. But the man was big, and he was strong. He turned around.

Clarissa saw Hope hanging onto the back of the man. He went to shake her off, but he was struggling as Hope worked her hand around his neck. He was then hit from the front. A blonde-haired figure, throwing punches at him, but the man reached out with a hand, slapping her aside.

200

Hope had slid off him, and was standing in front of Macleod and Clarissa. Cunningham had got back up off the floor, as the man turned and looked at them. Behind him, fire raged in the room. There were screams. The man looked round, and could hear the cries of 'police'. He flung the machete away, into the room behind him, and turned and ran.

Clarissa saw Hope turn and grab Macleod. 'Seoras, are you all right? Seoras.' There was blood on his wounds, sick down his front from where he'd vomited and he appeared to have blacked out.

'Ambulance. He was alive. When I cut him down, he was alive. Get him an ambulance,' said Clarissa.

Hope picked Macleod up and strode from the room. Susan Cunningham took hold of Clarissa, hauling her up on her feet.

'Got to get out of here.'

Together, the pair of women followed Hope as she raced out through the burning fire. There were now police around, and as they stepped outside, Clarissa was ushered to one side with Cunningham.

'Did you see where he went?' asked Clarissa. 'The man in the grey, the man in the mask.'

The uniformed constable looked back at her. 'There're loads of people in masks. They're all in grey. They're everywhere.'

Chapter 25

'How is he?'

The question was a simple one, and yet Hope believed there must be some complexity in the answer. She had just received a call from Jim, the Assistant Chief Constable, and he was too early with the call. He had known she was dropping in to see Macleod, but she originally quoted a time that was an hour earlier. Her paperwork and a lot of detail about what had gone on with Clarissa had come back to bite her and she was only now about to walk in the door.

'Sorry, Jim. I haven't seen him yet. I'm just outside the convalescence home. It's quite nice actually, isn't it?'

'I thought he deserved the best, so I pulled a few strings. I don't think I've ever seen somebody take quite a beating like that, especially when they've no idea why they're getting it.'

'I have no idea either,' said Hope. 'It makes little sense, but as a team, we'll be investigating it.'

'Of course, but look after the rest of the team as well. It's been rough and as far as we know, the guy that orchestrated all of this is still on the loose.'

'Well, we've gone through the rest of them. We've taken in

what they've said. By the looks of it, he had reached out to people who had suffered. He was quite the motivator. Coaxed them all to partake in this. He could identify people with a dark side in them, the susceptible ones. The ones for whom he could paint justice in doing all they did. He'd started small with the ministers. Now he was onto the financial sector, but things didn't go as well. There are few people who can keep up such a pretence without someone getting lucky against them. But to have a go at us, that was vicious.'

'Was that just to throw you off the case? Was that him just trying to say back off?' asked Jim.

'I'm not so sure,' said Hope. 'I'm hoping we'll get answers on that. In the meantime, I've asked for increased vigilance and security. We've knocked this guy for six, but we haven't put him down yet. He's not knocked out.'

'No, of course not, but I'll let you get on,' said Jim. 'Pass on my best wishes to him.'

'Of course,' said Hope. She closed down the call and strode forward onto the steps that led into the convalescence home. It was by the sea which Macleod would've liked, she thought. His own home overlooked the Moray Firth, though whether that would still be their home when they went back, who knew?

Jane had just been shot there. She'd been chased by a rabble before in that location as well, Hope coming to her rescue. This seemed worse than before.

Hope approached the front desk where a kindly woman in white smiled up at her.

'Detective Inspector Hope McGrath, I'm here to see DCI Macleod. That's Seoras Macleod.'

'Mr Macleod is not really himself today. Well, he hasn't been since he came in. He's a bit off-kilter to what he used to be, at least according to his wife. She's in here as well now, just on a basic recovery. With him out of the picture, I believe a decision was made for her to take some time out here. Maybe we should go see her first. I believe you're the junior in the team?'

I'm a bloody detective inspector, thought Hope. *I'm not a junior. I'm no junior in the team.*

Hope followed the woman anyway, and she passed down a long corridor until they reached a room.

'There's a splendid view out onto the sea beyond. Mrs Macleod is just over . . .'

'I know who Mrs Macleod is,' said Hope. 'I can see Jane, so I'll make my own way over. No problem talking to her, I take it.'

'No, no. Like I say, she's just having some basic recovery.'

Hope walked across past several people who were asleep or engaged in some quiet relaxation. She reached a window where Jane sat in a large seat, looking out to sea.

'Don't get up,' said Hope.

'Don't worry, I won't.'

'How are you?'

'I'm okay,' said Jane. 'The surgeons have done their work. I'm going to be a few months getting stronger, but I'm out of the woods. There's no reason they say why I shouldn't get back on my feet in time and carry on with life, but it was close.'

'So I believe. How's Seoras?'

'Physically, he's tough, given his age, and he keeps going. He'll be back up on his feet. The wounds will heal, although at the moment they're still smarting. But mentally, I've never seen him like this. He's lost that edge. Dear God, I hope the nightmares leave him. They beat him to a pulp.

'I sat with him last night and all he said was, "Why?" He kept reiterating to me, "I did nothing. I've done nothing." Asked if I believed him. Of course, I do. This is Seoras.

'"Mary Smith," he said. "Who's Mary Smith? I don't know a Mary Smith." He's been waking up in the night as well. They won't let me go into him at night. They tell me I have to have my rest, but during the day I'll see him, especially if he's very agitated. He's calmer with me. When you see him, be aware,' said Jane, 'that's not Seoras yet. He's not fully back. I hope he can come back from this. I'm not sure. I'm really not sure, Hope.'

Hope watched as the woman cried. She bent down, reducing her six-feet frame down to Jane's height in the seat and took the woman in her arms. She held her as Jane cried on her shoulder. After a few moments, she broke off, pushed herself back into the chair, and allowed Hope to stand.

'He would tell me anything, Hope. You understand that, anything. Even things he would do wrong, he would tell me. He's telling me nothing. I don't understand this. He talks a lot about the early days since he went away. The surrounding people, he has suspicions, he says, but not the way Seoras normally talks. Normally, he'd be incisive by backing up his opinion. You know how he is.'

Hope nodded.

'But he says he can't see it. He can't see who would have done something back then. Can't see why. So he doesn't understand why they took him. Why anyone would want revenge from back then? The few things that were covered up, they came out. The man hiding in Scalpay. He said, find out for me, Jane. It isn't a wife he needs now for that. He needs his colleagues. But you went and got him. I'll never be able to thank you enough for that.'

'He'd come for us,' said Hope. 'We'd come for you, too.'

'I know,' said Jane. 'I know. I need to take my walk. I don't walk far, but I have to do my exercise every day. Have to build my strength up. I'm told I have to look after myself, too. Not to put too much undue stress on me with the way Seoras is. How do you say that to a wife? How do you expect her to handle that?'

'You'll handle it the way you always do. Straight up, you'll do what you need to do, Jane. You're going to lift his mood. You're his world.'

'I'm his at-home world and, don't get me wrong, I'm more than happy about that. But when he goes right to work, you, Ross, Clarissa, the rest of them, the force, that's his world. That's what's falling apart, not me, not us. We're fine. He's battered. He's in a mess, but we're fine. Don't have any concerns about that. Find me what's going on, Hope. Find me what's bugging my Seoras. Tell me why they're coming for him.'

'Will do,' said Hope.

'Remember, he trusted you. You're the one he raves about. You're the one he gets most disappointed in if you do something wrong because he thinks you're the best. He only cares that way about those he thinks are really good; the others just have to learn. Go, find out what's happening with him.'

Hope watched Jane stand up. She was fairly steady on her feet, but clearly, she was tired. She walked out of the room unaided and Hope, on leaving, saw her approaching a room with a door. Hope stood for a moment, then watched Jane emerge in her coat and disappear off outside.

No one had told her where Seoras was, so she walked back to

the desk. They pointed down the corridor, telling her to take two rights. It was number seventeen. Hope walked corridors that looked pleasant, but to her, as much as you tried to dress it up as a home, it was still a hospital of sorts. Still, better in here than a sharp, cold ward with disinfectant everywhere.

Hope arrived and knocked on the door of seventeen, which was lying open. Inside, a man was sprawled on the bed. He looked weary, lying in pyjamas with a paisley design.

'Seoras.' Macleod opened his eyes. 'Hey, Seoras. It's me. It's Hope.'

Slowly, the eyes blinked, and then he sat up. Hope could tell it was an effort to do so. He turned around on the bed, so his feet swung off. He looked over at her, almost distant in some ways, and tried to stand to come over to her. She saw him go to fall and swept him up, sweeping her arms under his.

'Let's get you back on the bed. Come on.'

She made Macleod lie down again and pulled the chair up beside the bed to be beside him.

'You worried me this time, worried me. You got Clarissa to thank, but you knew that, didn't you? Seoras let her go digging, turned the Rottweiler loose.'

There was a faint smile etching across his face and then a gentle nod of the head. But then his face went suddenly grey, his features tightening, agitation beginning in his limbs. He cried, his body shaking.

'Hope,' he said in a gravelly voice. 'Hope, they beat me. They whipped me. They were going to evis . . . evis . . . if I couldn't tell them.'

'Eviscerate,' said Hope flatly.

'Yes,' he said. 'Slice me open. Kept asking me—who is she? Who's Mary Smith? Who's Mary Smith?'

Suddenly, he was bolt upright in the bed, sweat pouring down his face.

'I don't know who she is. There's no Mary Smith. We don't know a Mary Smith. They don't mean Mairi. They don't mean Mairi Smith. I knew Mairi, I don't know Mary. Stornoway, they said. They said it's back in Stornoway. I don't understand.'

Hope reached forward and threw her arms around him. She held him tight.

'Hush,' she said. 'Seoras, hush. We'll find out. We'll get to the bottom of it.'

For a moment, he continued to shake, and then it stopped. He leaned back away from Hope, and suddenly there was a smile on his face.

'Where's Clarissa?' he said. 'We must get her back. She needs to come back to the team. Did you . . .'

'Did I what?' asked Hope.

'Did you manage to . . . well, sweep it all under the carpet.'

'Had to say she was undercover,' said Hope. 'Jim did it. He suggested it. A good man. He took her in to his office and tore her out about going rogue. She shouldn't have done this and she shouldn't have done that. To which she said, 'You would be dead without it.' Every time Jim said something, she had a reply for him. When she left, she hadn't said if she was coming back. She said she had something to find out. Something she needed to know.

Macleod stood up. Hope saw him wince, turn, and took a step to the window. Hope stood behind him, looking out.

'Nice view,' she said.

'Over the water,' said Macleod. 'She's going for answers over the water. She suspects everyone,' he said. 'That's why she's so good. That's why you send her in. When things look dodgy.

Not afraid of anyone. Prepared to stand up. Doesn't need to climb the ladder.'

'Do you think she'll be back?' Hope asked him.

'Depends what she finds in Stornoway.' Macleod gave her a raw chuckle.

'Okay,' said Hope. 'I'll wait then.'

'You'll probably hear about it first,' said Macleod. 'Some complaint.'

* * *

The lady that showed her into the Leverburgh nursing home had a face like a smacked arse. At least that's how Clarissa would tell it. Someday, she should tell them about coming in here and about the woman that had guided her into the room. Maybe she just had a bad day, who knew.

McNeil was sitting on his own, a coffee in front of him, a Bible sitting on the armchair. There was a younger woman in there, too, and she at least turned and smiled at Clarissa. Not everyone could have had a face like the woman that greeted her, if indeed it was a greeting.

'McNeil,' said Clarissa.

'Urquhart,' he said, the contempt in his voice. 'You could at least have dressed like a police officer.'

'Don't even begin to piss me about,' said Clarissa. 'I'm here for one reason—Mary Smith. Who the hell is Mary Smith?'

'Mary Smith was a woman who came to the station. She claimed she'd been out on the road. Someone had stopped in a car, taking a shine to her. Asked her to get in. She had refused. He had got out and over the next hour and a half, he'd subjected Mary to his will.'

'We were there, me, Anderson, Clark, Beaton, Macleod,' continued McNeil. 'The five of us were in, but the others didn't deal with it. They saw her come in and they directed her to me. Hysterical woman. She was saying very little, but once inside the room, I was able to find out. Told me every detail.'

'And,' said Clarissa, 'you did what?'

'Understand, at the time, there were some difficulties within a few congregations. There was one man bringing them together. One good man, but a man who also had certain desires. His wife had taken enough of his perversions from him. Mary was unfortunate enough to be subject to them.

'I wasn't unkind to her. I got her a job on the mainland. She went two weeks later. I checked up on her after the first year and a half. She was doing well. She had a good life. If she had stayed, there's always those people who would have said that she had encouraged him. I made the best of the situation. We couldn't have had the church disrupted.'

Clarissa looked at the cup of coffee in front of McNeil. She bent down, painful as it was because of her bumps and bruises from the previous days.

'You had a woman come to you for help, having endured something like that, and you had her shipped off the island?'

'Sometimes you need a pragmatic approach. God's work has to be done. It needed a fix, and we had the man to do it. There are priorities. I kept the rest of them out of it. They thought she was just mad. Daft. A hysterical woman. Sometimes, you got to think what's the best way to protect his work. You got to think how he should be uplifted.'

Clarissa felt numb. 'And Macleod,' she said, 'he was there with you.'

'Ian Seoras Macleod was with us. A young constable who didn't last very long. Had a career of about fifteen months. Just after that incident, in came Seoras Macleod, your friend. He had nothing to do with Mary Smith.'

Clarissa felt her hands begin to tremble and shake.

'They almost killed him for this. They almost killed him,' she said. 'If I hadn't got to him, he was dead. You have a cheek? You have the gall to talk about doing what's right for God?'

'A heathen like you wouldn't understand,' said McNeil. He turned his eyes down, looking away from Clarissa. She got the feeling he thought of her as a piece of what the dog leaves behind on the pavement.

Clarissa picked up his coffee cup and spat into it, slamming it down on the table in front of him.

'I may not understand,' she said, 'but there's a man who prides himself on being one of God's and he would've rounded on you for what you just told me. Even this woeful sinner,' she said, pointing to herself, 'can see the evil in what you did. You should have taken that whipping. They should have taken you in.'

'Macleod would understand,' said McNeil. 'We need to keep the church upright.'

'Macleod would never understand what you just said. That's why he's my friend.'

She turned on her heel, walked out of the room. Clarissa felt bad when the rather cheerful worker gave her a smile and she didn't smile back. She felt less annoyed when she walked past the grumpy woman and stepped outside the care home.

Clarissa walked over to the edge of the car park and looked out at the small loch in front of her. The water was rippling. She picked up her mobile phone and placed a call to Frank.

She'd done badly by him. His new wife had torn off to sort out her friends and work, to sort out her police colleagues, and not involve him. She'd decided it was safer, but she had been wrong. Not that he would've come with her, but at least he would've understood.

'It's Frank, love. How did it go?'

'Got things to do, Frank. Things to do. Just wait for me, okay?'

'Okay, Clarissa,' he said. She could have kissed him for that.

Read on to discover the Patrick Smythe series!

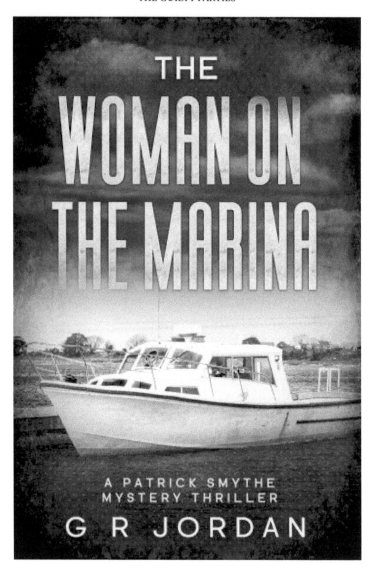

THE

WOMAN ON
THE MARINA

A PATRICK SMYTHE
MYSTERY THRILLER

G R JORDAN

Patrick Smythe is a former Northern Irish policeman who

after suffering an amputation after a bomb blast, takes to the sea between the west coast of Scotland and his homeland to ply his trade as a private investigator. Join Paddy as he tries to work to his own ethics while knowing how to bend the rules he once enforced. Working from his beloved motorboat 'Craigantlet', Paddy decides to rescue a drug mule in this short story from the pen of G R Jordan.

Join G R Jordan's monthly newsletter about forthcoming releases and special writings for his tribe of avid readers and then receive your free Patrick Smythe short story.

Go to https://bit.ly/PatrickSmythe for your Patrick Smythe journey to start!

About the Author

GR Jordan is a self-published author who finally decided at forty that in order to have an enjoyable lifestyle, his creative beast within would have to be unleashed. His books mirror that conflict in life where acts of decency contend with self-promotion, goodness stares in horror at evil, and kindness blindsides us when we at our worst. Corrupting our world with his parade of wondrous and horrific characters, he highlights everyday tensions with fresh eyes whilst taking his methodical, intelligent mainstays on a roller-coaster ride of dilemmas, all the while suffering the banter of their provoca-tive sidekicks.

A graduate of Loughborough University where he masquer-aded as a chemical engineer but ultimately played American football, Gary had worked at changing the shape of cereal flakes and pulled a pallet truck for a living. Watching vegetables freeze at -40'C was another career highlight and he was also one of the Scottish Highlands "blind" air traffic controllers. These days he has graduated to answering a telephone to people in trouble before telephoning other people to sort it out.

Having flirted with most places in the UK, he is now based in the Isle of Lewis in Scotland where his free time is spent between raising a young family with his wife, writing, figuring out how to work a loom and caring for a small flock of chickens. Luckily, his writing is influenced by his varied work and life experience as the chickens have not been the poetical inspiration he had hoped for!

You can connect with me on:
🌐 https://grjordan.com
📘 https://facebook.com/carpetlessleprechaun

Subscribe to my newsletter:
✉ https://bit.ly/PatrickSmythe

Also by G R Jordan

G R Jordan writes across multiple genres including crime, dark and action adventure fantasy, feel good fantasy, mystery thriller and horror fantasy. Below is a selection of his work. Whilst all books are available across online stores, signed copies are available at his personal shop.

Vengeance is Mine! (Highlands & Islands Detective Book 28)
Messages passed to a policeman in hospice care. Apocalyptic tales found in notes in his room. Is Macleod losing his mind as well as his health, or is there one last hurrah for a familiar foe?

When Seoras Macleod believes he sees an horrific figure from the recent past he puts it down to a state of PTSD. But when the evidence at his care facility seems to confirm the visits of a recent killer, he cannot shake off the feeling that he is being warned of a disaster of the murderer's making. Will the team trust their old mentor when he seems to be losing his mind?

With old age comes wisdom, and not a little insanity!

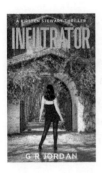

Infiltrator (A Kirsten Stewart Thriller #10)

https://grjordan.com/product/infiltrator

Secrets being leaked from an overseas embassy. A mole too clever to be fooled by standard red herrings. Can Kirsten keep herself alive and find the mole before he discovers her cover?

Back in the pay of the British secret services, Kirsten must travel to South America where secrets are being passed through a mole known only as 'The Goldsmith'. But as Kirsten unearths the true nature of the information being passed, she finds herself in a race against time to stop a dirty bomb that goes right for the heart of British society.

The countdown has begun!

Jac's Revenge (A Jack Moonshine Thriller #1)

An unexpected hit makes Debbie a widow. The attention of her man's killer spawns a brutal yet classy alter ego. But how far can you play the game before it takes over your life?

All her life, Debbie Parlor lived in her man's shadow, knowing his work was never truly honest. She turned her head from news stories and rumours. But when he was disposed of for his smile to placate a rival crime lord, Jac Moonshine was born. And when Debbie is paid compensation for her loss like her car was written off, Jac decides that enough is enough.

Get on board with this tongue-in-cheek revenge thriller that will make you question how far you would go to avenge a loved one, and how much you would enjoy it!

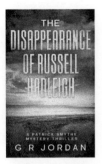

The Disappearance of Russell Hadleigh (Patrick Smythe Book 1)

https://grjordan.com/product/the-disappearance-of-russell-hadleigh

A retired judge fails to meet his golf partner. His wife calls for help while running a fantasy play ring. When Russians start co-opting into a fairly-traded clothing brand, can Paddy untangle the strands before the bodies start littering the golf course?

In his first full novel, Patrick Smythe, the single-armed former policeman, must infiltrate the golfing social scene to discover the fate of his client's husband. Assisted by a young starlet of the greens, Paddy tries to understand just who bears a grudge and who likes to play in the rough, culminating in a high stakes showdown where lives are hanging by the reaction of a moment. If you love pacey action, suspicious motives and devious characters, then Paddy Smythe operates amongst your kind of people.

Love is a matter of taste but money always demands more of its suitor.

Milton Keynes UK
Ingram Content Group UK Ltd.
UKHW031115080824
446563UK00001B/28